SMOKE
on the
WATER

Other Books by John Ruemmler:

Brothers in Arms
Night of the Nazgul
Rangers of the North

SMOKE
on the
WATER

**A Novel of Jamestown
and the Powhatans**

John Ruemmler

SHOE TREE PRESS
WHITE HALL, VIRGINIA

Published by Shoe Tree Press, an imprint of
Betterway Publications, Inc.
P.O. Box 219
Crozet, VA 22932
(804) 823-5661

Cover design by Rick Britton
Captain John Smith's map reproduced through the
courtesy of the Virginia Historical Society.
Typography by Park Lane Associates

Library of Congress Cataloging-in-Publication Data

Ruemmler, John
    Smoke on the water : a novel of Jamestown and the
Powhatans / John Ruemmler.
        p. cm.
    Includes bibliographical references (p.) and index.
    Summary: Near Jamestown in 1622, a young English boy
and the son of a Powhatan Indian chief find themselves
caught up in the growing animosity between their peoples.
    ISBN 1-55870-239-3 (hardcover) : $12.95
    1. Jamestown (Va.)--History--Juvenile fiction. [1.
Jamestown (Va.)--History--Fiction. 2. Powhatan Indians--
Fiction. 3. Indians of North America--Virginia--Fiction.]
    I. Title.
PZ7.R88534Sm 1992
[Fic]--dc20   91-42587
                                                      CIP
                                                       AC

Printed in the United States of America
0 9 8 7 6 5 4 3 2 1

To Jessica and Adam, daughter and son,
Rainbow and Thunder
You make a playground of the planet!

Thanks, Daddy-O

ACKNOWLEDGMENTS

Special thanks to Nancy Egloff, Staff Historian at the Jamestown Settlement, and to Shelly Napier.

CONTENTS

Chapter 1. A Fight in the Forest   **11**

Chapter 2. Eagle Owl's Dream   **41**

Chapter 3. The Wrestling Match   **55**

Chapter 4. The Rival   **83**

Chapter 5. The Witch's Daughter   **93**

Chapter 6. Exiled   **105**

Chapter 7. The Power of Gold   **115**

Chapter 8. The Huskanaw   **133**

Chapter 9. The Massacre   **149**

Chapter 10. Wandering Warriors   **165**

Bibliography   **173**

A NOTE TO THE READER

The central characters of this book are fictional. However genuine their emotions and actions, the Spencers of Jamestown as well as Eagle Owl and his Powhatan (or Algonkian) family are creations of imagination. Other characters who play a minor role in the events are real: Governor Thomas Wyatt, for example, and Opechancanough (leader of the Powhatans) walked the land and sailed the rivers of Virginia in the 1620s, and they fought each other after the "Massacre" of 1622. The author of historical fiction spins a tale he makes up in order to get at the truth: what life was really like for two boys and their families, one English and one Algonkian, over 350 years ago.

Chapter One

A FIGHT IN THE FOREST

Whitsunday was a fortnight in the past, and Easter—a day when the sun danced in the sky—was nine weeks gone. Three-inch high tobacco seedlings had been planted by the thousands in the fields outside the fort. Watered and weeded and pampered like gold pieces growing in the earth, the tobacco plants drew the men and indentured servants of Jamestown to the edge of the Indian woods every day, from May until the harvest in September. When the dried tobacco leaf was packed in barrels and shipped to England in October, Jamestown would rejoice: men would have the credit to buy new hoes and boots, women might purchase bolts of cloth for a new gown and a new iron cooking pot. For the children, shoes with shiny buckles, whalebone combs, and a broad-brimmed felt hat to keep the sun away became more than just a dream.

Today, Thomas begged his father's pardon and after a half-day of killing weeds in the tobacco fields, ran to the thickets near the swamp. He picked the wild strawberries as his mother had taught him, bending low to the bush and pulling free the stem while holding the plump berry in his hand like a jewel. He had almost filled the wooden bucket. Nowhere in England had he seen such red, juicy berries. Some were nearly as big as his fist! He plucked one free of the bush and bit into it, letting the sweet pink juice dribble down his chin and fall to the earth. The crisp, pimpled skin of the berry tickled his tongue and soothed his parched throat. Thomas liked the Virginia summer thus far and could not fathom the dread that Jamestown's men and women had of the season. Hadn't the Starving Time been the *winter* of 1610, now eleven years past? Why fear the summer, when the berry bushes drooped with fruit and the wildflowers perfumed the air like royalty on a stroll through the wildwood?

He heard a tapping farther in the woods, deeper in Indian territory, like someone knocking at a door. A woodpecker. His favorite bird in all of the new and strange world, the woodpecker earned his food by rapping at tree trunks and snatching the fleeing insects with ease. Less than one foot tall, the redheaded bird raised a racket that a man with a sharp axe and two strong arms was challenged to match. Thomas wondered that the hungry bird never got a headache, using his head like a hammer all the day long. Matthew Garret was like that—hardheaded—and had won many a wrestling match by knocking his opponent unconscious with that iron noggin of his. Maybe way back Matthew had a redheaded woodpecker for a relation. Thomas laughed at his jest; the sound of his laughter carried through the forest like the cry of a strange bird.

Sunlight filtered through the tall pines and warmed the forest floor at his feet. Vines twisted and curled like crude green lace and sent up little white flowers so tiny he feared to touch them. Pausing to listen for the woodpecker's rapping deeper in the woods, Thomas wiped the sweat and dust from his forehead. He was determined to go home with a bucket full of berries. His father called him "Halfway-Thomas" because he sometimes failed to complete a chore or forgot it entirely; today he would give his father no cause for complaint. Testing his strength, he lifted the bucket by the thick rope handle; he could barely walk upright while lugging the berries between his knees, and his arms were all but pulled out of their sockets by the weight.

"Twenty pounds or I'm a pirate!" he cried out, proud of himself. Wouldn't Mother be pleased? Somewhere off in the woods, a blackbird squawked. Overhead, two squirrels gave chase, crying foul and leaping from limb to limb of a giant oak tree that scraped the blue dome of heaven. A twig fell at Thomas's feet, the handiwork of the scampering squirrels. Playfully, he shook his fist at them before bending to the task once more. A bluejay scolded him and wished him gone.

Thomas had just palmed a plump beauty fit for the palate of King James when something hit him square in the back of the head. *Thonk*! Instinctively, he ducked, cowering behind the strawberry bush and searching for the source of what had hit him. Was it a rock? It was surely hard. He felt the back of his head with his fingers but they came back with no blood on them. He listened intently for the crack of a twig or the crackle of dry leaves underfoot but heard nothing, just the distant rapping of the woodpecker and from the edge of the forest, near Jamestown, the *chink* of William Johnson's axe biting at the trunk of a tree. On the ground at his feet he spied a strawberry, one that he swore he did not pick. It was smaller than those in the wood bucket and pale at the tip, unripened, and hard as a stone to the touch. Again Thomas felt with his fingers and found a small knot rising from the back of his skull. Who had flung the unripe berry at him? Why?

Thomas suspected Matthew Garret, but he tromped through the woods like a bull and could be heard for miles, terrifying wild turkeys and flushing all game out of the area long before he had the chance to take aim. No, it wasn't Matthew. Whoever hit him with the rock-hard berry had good aim and was quiet as a fox. Who else could it be?

Thomas raised his head above the bush to have a look around. He saw a flash to the east, a glint of metal by the river, before something hit him flush in the forehead. The *thonk*! he heard sounded like a musket ball rattling around inside his head; the blow sent him reeling to the ground. Dizzy, Thomas lay on his back, stunned, and gasped for air. His heart raced. He looked up through the lace of leaves to see lazy clouds slipping by and almost blacked out. A titter from the meadow's eastern edge snapped him awake. Who was laughing? His persecutor? Why?

Thomas raised his head and squinted, peering toward the river, and saw nothing untoward. Though his heart was racing and his head ached, he sensed no real danger. If the Algonkians wanted him, they could have taken him weeks ago, in the late spring, when he passed long days beside his father, planting tobacco in the cleared fields outside the town walls. Giving up on solving yet another small mystery in the new world, he rubbed his forehead and resolved to tell his father about the incident without delay. Wiping away the sweat of fear, he kneeled in the dirt and felt for another ripe strawberry. His forehead throbbed, as if a little creature were inside struggling to get out.

A hand grabbed him by the collar and pulled him backward, choking him for a moment. Thomas cried out and squirmed free, getting to his feet with his fists cocked. A grinning Indian boy about his size but wider at the shoulders stood two feet away, waiting for Thomas to do something. The Indian had no weapon and wore only the loincloth and bead necklace so favored by the savages. His eyes were dark and gleamed with mischief. The feathers in his hair and dangling earrings marked him as a chief's son or nephew, for all Thomas had heard. The savage made a motion, nodding to the basket of berries, then looked back at Thomas, who was puzzled and a little wary. What did he want, a wrestling match? The strawberries? The bucket? Thomas wasn't giving them up without a fight. He shook his head and waved the boy off.

"Go on now!" Thomas said, brave as he could sound. "Go!"

Quicker than a copperhead, the young Indian snatched a strawberry from the basket. Grinning, he turned and threw it at the trunk of an oak tree twenty feet away, where it hit and exploded. The savage laughed and bent down to get another. Thomas grabbed his hand to prevent him.

"That's my food," he said, knowing the savage did not understand him. "Stop!"

At Thomas's warning, the boy threw back his head and laughed, showing a mouthful of white teeth. He wrenched free of Thomas's grip by twisting his wrist until, wincing, Thomas had to let go. The boy snatched and ate two berries, then two more, until his jaws were swollen and pink juice ran freely down his chin. The Indian's dark eyes were merry, and his feet moved back and forth across the forest floor in a rhythm Thomas had seen at one of the Algonkian ceremonies of welcome.

One by one, he's going to take all the berries, Thomas realized. With a shove, he knocked the Indian boy onto his rump and grabbed the bucket. He ran south, toward the swamp and Jamestown, keeping the river at his right shoulder. Jumping over a fallen log, Thomas tripped and dropped the bucket. Strawberries rolled out onto the ground. Before he could get to his feet, the Indian was upon him. They rolled in the vines and brush, gripping each other by an arm or the hair, grunting like wild boars. A sharp twig stuck Thomas in the cheek, and he cried out. That quick, the Indian released him and pulled him to his feet. Thomas flinched, but the boy pushed his hand away and felt where the twig had gouged a hole in Thomas's cheek. The young Indian's eyes showed concern, not anger. He dragged and shoved Thomas down to the shady banks of the river fifty feet away. While Thomas twisted away to free himself, he slapped mud on the bloody cheek. The pain subsided; the cool mud soothed the hurt.

Thomas was bewildered: first he near to kills me, then he helps me. Savages!

The sun burned down on them. Thomas tried to get to his feet once, to gather the bucket and berries and be on his way back home, but the Indian boy would not allow him free passage and held him down. The boy's grip was strong; his fingers left their mark on Thomas's arm. So they sat with their feet in the cool mud of the river bank, the heat of the sun baking the tops of their heads, gnats buzzing in their ears, waiting for Thomas knew not what. The thought went through his mind like an arrow that he was being held captive, but why? He was not the Governor's son or the firstborn of a nobleman. Like a hundred others, his father grew tobacco and built cabins. Of what value was Thomas to Old Powhatan's untamed folk? None.

As they sat quietly, the sluggish brown current carried past them branches and other reminders of the first storm of the summer. Then Thomas saw a strange sight. In the shallows of a bend in the river there appeared a half-dozen Indians, full-grown warriors in loincloths and beads. He did not know whether they had been watching Thomas's struggle or even noticed the boys two hundred feet away, partially hidden by overhanging branches and dense shrubs.

The Indians lifted large stones and great oak limbs and tossed them into the shallows of the river with a splash. By bracing one with the other, they had soon erected a U-shaped barrier extending open-mouthed twenty feet into the sluggish current. Thomas wondered what they meant to do next. Having created a crude barrier, they began to fill it with roots, bark, and horse-chestnuts. The water soon boiled around the Indians' feet. Fish leapt to escape suffocation, and with practiced ease, the warriors caught striped bass and silvery shad and a sheepshead with their bare hands, sometimes in mid-leap. They tossed the river's bounty ashore and, in a few moments, had a booty of twenty good-sized fish flapping and twisting on the shady banks of the King's River. It took them but a moment or two to toss their catch into a large woven basket, which two of the Algonkians lifted.

What an uncivilized way to fish, Thomas thought. He was convinced that the savages had not noticed them until the last one to get out of the water paused for a moment and raised an arm in the boys' direction; Thomas's nemesis returned the greeting in silence, and the Indians quickly disappeared into the woods on the western shore of the river.

Without a sound, the boy sprinkled water on Thomas's face, washing away the mud. He peered intently at the wound, nodded solemnly, and turned away. Then the savage did a strange thing: he rose on the balls of his feet and stretched his arms as if soaring in the sky. He circled Thomas with his arms open wide and cried like a hawk before coming to roost beside the puzzled English boy. The Indian pointed to himself and said something Thomas could not understand. Then he realized that the savage was "telling" him his name: Hawk. Or Eagle. Indians had names like that, he knew, not Christian names like "Thomas" or "Andrew."

How do I act out "Thomas," he wondered? The Indian pointed at him and waited. Thomas looked back blankly and shrugged his shoulders. The Indian looked bewildered and scratched his head. The boy pointed once more at Thomas's chest, then gave up. They walked back to the spilled berries; after helping Thomas pick up the spilt berries, the Indian boy easily lifted the bucket.

Thomas quickly spoke all the Indian words he knew: "Squash, skunk, canoe, moccasin ..."

Delighted, the Indian boy laughed and danced in a circle, spinning with the bucket in his hands. Thomas thought he was going to steal the berries and the bucket, but instead his persecutor stopped and set down the bucket, again with the solemn face so common to the savages of Virginia. In the earth at their feet, the Indian made a mark with a sharp stick, a curving line like a half-circle. The symbol reminded Thomas of a hunting bow, or perhaps a rainbow, or a bridge over a stream. He was puzzled; the boy could not explain. He stood solemn and silent, his gaze directed at the sign. Thomas took his concentration to mean that the drawing meant something special to him or to all the Algonkians, and after pausing for a respectful moment, Thomas lifted the bucket and headed for home, keeping the river over his right shoulder. He turned around once to see where the berry-thief was, but he, like his elders, had disappeared into the forest with that gift of silence that all Indians had. Like the fox, they vanished at will into the woods.

🐦 🐦 🐦

Perspiration obscured his view; the salt from his sweat stung his lips. The rope handle of the bucket bit into his hands until they bled. The long solitary walk back to Jamestown while carrying the bucket full of strawberries was a bad idea. But he wanted to show his father that he could complete a task to perfection and ached to please his mother, who suffered so with fevers that on most hot days, she arose from bed only to weed the garden and the grave, feed the chickens and cow, and cook meals. His shoulders were stiff and burned with fatigue. His mouth was dry as leaves, and his throat parched. When Thomas paused to catch his breath outside the Garret cottage, who should appear to taunt him but Matthew the Stonehead himself. For a lad of fourteen, Matthew was almost a man's size, with powerful shoulders and arms but a pea-sized mind. His lips were permanently formed into a scowl, and if he ever smiled, Thomas wasn't there to see it. Matthew folded his arms and sneered.

"Hey, berry-girl! Mother's bucket-boy, are you now?"

Ignoring the Stonehead, who growled at him from the thatch overhang of the doorway, Thomas politely asked for a drink of well water and was obliged by Matthew's mother, who appeared on the porch to scold her son and ask about Thomas's mother. He said she was fine, which wasn't really a lie, for she would be well when the heat lifted and the cool autumn winds blew down from the western mountains. Then she would rise with the sun and make meals and, in the evenings, mend their garments by rushlight. When the autumn sun grew warm, she would churn butter on the porch and greet the planters and indentured servants walking to and from the tobacco fields where the cultivated lands of the English met the tall green wall of woods, which the Algonkians ruled. Those days were coming, Thomas knew, once the heat of summer withdrew.

The cool water slaked his thirst. Mrs. Garret looked on kindly. Her husband, Matthew's father, was a bricklayer employed by Gentleman Martin, who was building a grand manor house of brick and wood downriver, a house worthy of an English gentleman. From under the broad brim of her straw hat her merry blue eyes sparkled; Thomas wondered how Matthew had managed to shun all of his mother's kindness and most of his father's dexterity. You'd think some of it would seep under his skin and soften his heart, but no. Matthew had the Pharaoh's heart, hard and unforgiving as stone. Thomas was about to thank Mrs. Garret for the drink when she glimpsed his hands.

"Gracious! Your hands need salving," she said simply. Smiling, she went inside, wiping her hands on the cloth apron that hung from her waist to her ankles. The turkey feather in the brim of her hat gave Mrs. Garret a jaunty air that some village women found distasteful, but no one accused her of being less than a pious woman and a worthy friend. Thomas's mother called her "my worthy sister," the greatest of compliments to someone who was not kin.

With his mother gone inside, Matthew stepped forward, glaring. "What's that knot on your head?" His voice was gruff and low, his father's voice at a slightly higher pitch. The muscles in his forearms knotted like thick vines as he crossed his arms.

Thomas felt the bump on his forehead with his fingers; it must be the size of a strawberry, he figured. What would he tell his father and mother? He said nothing.

"Come Court Day, I'll give you a bigger welt!" Matthew threatened, and he meant it. He banged his fist into his palm with a resounding smack. "You can't hide from me no more!" He squinted his pig's eyes at Thomas, trying to look even more terrifying.

Every month, the men and their near-to-grown sons met for a day at the Courthouse to buy and sell tobacco and livestock, argue about their representatives here and in England, and debate the danger posed by Powhatan's folk now that their great chief was dead and a peace had been stamped in brass on an oak tree by the Governor. Before organizing into a militia and marching to and fro with their muskets on their shoulders, men swapped tall tales about gold and silver mines a hundred miles to the west, where the mountains were said to stand blue in the morning's haze. The men of Jamestown who owned land were supposed to drill as militia regularly, but the threat from Spaniards down south didn't seem real and the Indians came and went as they pleased without incident. As Thomas had learned, there hadn't been a shooting war for years, since Pocahontas was a girl cartwheeling through the dusty streets of the fort. A few wandering churls who kept to themselves and lived half the time with the savages might pipe up and say that the waves of the Indian Ocean lapped upon golden shores just on the other side of the blue mountains, and all the riches of China lay open to the men who claimed them, but Thomas knew of no man who had been there, and his father dismissed such talk as nonsense fueled by the Second Deadly Sin, covetousness.

On Court Day, the marching soon turned to shooting and wagering. Banns of marriage were nailed to the door of the clerk's office, next door to the jail. After a barrel of rum was wheeled out and tapped, some of the men and a few of the boys, like Matthew, wrestled for pleasure and prizes like tobacco or a new hatchet.

With a start of fear, his heart raced: Thomas knew he couldn't outmuscle Matthew and didn't know how to outwit him, so he hid when the challenges went forth through the throng of men and boys. He was ashamed, but not as much as he might be if he was pinned and maybe hurt by Matthew, who was a head taller and twice as broad at the shoulder. What good would he be to his parents with a broken arm? How could he weed and water and cut and carry firewood with one good arm? Or a broken skull? For some reason Thomas could not guess, Matthew wanted to wrestle *him* most of all. He wasn't the biggest or fastest boy in Jamestown, and he surely did not have the biggest mouth. Maybe it was because pretty Priscilla Powell smiled at Thomas when he passed the Powell cottage and would not raise her head at Matthew except to scowl and send him away like a mongrel dog. Matthew always looked at Priscilla as if she were a honeycomb dripping sweet nectar, but he was too tongue-tied even to say hello.

Where could he hide or run off to Court Day next, Thomas wondered, as Matthew's mother appeared at the door with a small wooden bowl. Mrs. Garret had apple-red cheeks and the smile of an angel. She handed her son a mended hoe and sent him off to the tobacco fields to join his father. With him went their indentured servant, a young Englishman named Wyther. In the two years he had served them, young Wyther had never looked a man in the eye, never spoken to anyone but Matthew's mother and father, and never raised his voice in jest or song, as far as Thomas knew. What was the fellow thinking, Thomas wondered, and how could he keep so silent?

Matthew eyed Thomas and mumbled a final threat before walking off to the west with Wyther, toward the tobacco mounds standing side by side across acre upon acre of cleared flatland.

"Indian herbs will heal those hands in good time," Mrs. Garret said, soothing the pain with her care and her voice. She dabbed the cool tart paste on his abrasions with her pale fingers. "Pay no heed to Matthew. He's full of phlegm and ought to be bled but he won't sit for it. The Lord is yet to teach him humility. The boy has a fire in his head, like his father. There!" She pronounced him well and sent him off with the bucket of berries. "Tell your mother I shall see her at the Church on the Sabbath."

Thomas nodded and thanked her again. Lifting the bucket, he noticed with great relief that the rope handles no longer caused him agony. He walked with a high heart down the path where puddles from yesterday's storm lay. He glanced back to see Matthew's mother sitting up straight on the wood bench that rested in the shade of the porch, needle in hand, sewing a shirt that must have belonged to her son. Thomas wished she might leave the needle in the collar to prick the conscience of his tormentor, then prayed for forgiveness for the evil thought. On he walked, past small stands of corn up to his waist and green fields of squash and peas. The twittering of hungry sparrows filled the air.

Abraham, Gentleman Hartley's Negro servant, walked by and nodded sullenly, his arms filled with shovels and hoes. He wore a linen shirt and dirty trousers and had neither boots nor a hat. His dark face shone with sweat. Thomas had watched him grind corn once; Abraham's muscles jumped with a life of their own. Somebody said he could wrestle a bear to a draw. Where had he come from?

"Africa." Thomas spoke the word aloud. It sounded dark, mysterious, and unChristian. There were only a few Negroes in Jamestown; the first had arrived in chains only two years before, in 1619.

Abraham passed him, the tools clattering in the black man's grip. Why did the man never smile? His chains were gone now. Why was his heart so sour, and was it really black, as Matthew said?

As the sun grew hotter and dust devils whipped about the dirt street, the few women of the village lingered in the shade of chestnut and oak trees, passing along local gossip, trading child-rearing do's and don't's, and swapping recipes for stews and soups. Living outside the high wooden fence that surrounded the heart of Jamestown, they seemed to fear nothing, trusting themselves and their families unto God's hands. So Thomas was told each time he asked his mother *why* new settlers—"new Comers," they were called—built crude wattle and daub cottages with no windows and a dirt floor and a fireplace that choked them with smoke. New Comers worked the land many miles from town, up the James as far as fifty miles, where the village of Henrico stood. They were surrounded by savages, woods, and the River, with the James their only means of escape. They had no fort to gather within during time of attack and no way to send for help in a timely fashion. They were truly alone in a way that Thomas found frightening, yet whenever he saw the men of Henrico at Court Day or, more rarely, at the Sabbath services, they appeared no more concerned about bloodthirsty Spanish pirates or warring Indians than were the Jamestowners.

They had some reason to be calm: peace had prevailed with the Algonkians for seven years. Three years and more had passed since Powhatan's death, and there was little sign of anger or alarm. The Indians were a part of everyday village life; they worked shoulder to shoulder with the English tobacco planters, they taught the English women how to heal wounds and cure fevers and grow corn and squash. Why would the Indians cause trouble? They had English tools and bangles; some hunted with English muskets, when the wet weather permitted the powder to burn. Powhatan's folk valued the English ax and knife; some slept with blankets shipped from England or cooked in iron pots. Algonkian men drank English rum and grew too fond of it. What more could they ask of the English, who had tamed the land and now raised tobacco and corn just as the Indians had taught them?

Like his father, Thomas had little to do with Powhatan's folk and granted them a native wisdom and happiness many Englishmen would do well to emulate. Since his encounter with the young savage near the wild strawberry patch, Thomas instinctively feared the Algonkians a little more. Like the twenty Africans who worked and lived in Jamestown, they baffled him. The inside of an Indian's half-shaved skull was virgin territory to him, unknown as the moon and just as unfathomable.

Still, some people were growing uneasy at the situation. At the last Court Day, Thomas overheard planters grumbling about Powhatan's successor, the new "King of the Algonkians," a Pamunkey chief who accused the English of seizing the richest farmland and pushing his people west and into the lair of their enemies, the Monacans. Such talk made the English uneasy; some planters carried their muskets to the fields with them, a precaution of earlier and more dangerous times. Thomas wondered who but God would make peace once and for all between the races, and when. His mother prayed for peace between the races and cited Jesus's commandment to love thy neighbor as thyself. But Thomas's father and most Englishmen did not consider the Algonkians to be neighbors; they viewed the Indians as savages—fallen creatures just a step above the beasts of the forest, a dark folk who worshipped and served evil spirits. Thomas knew nothing of that but shivered at the thought.

Sweating so much his vision was obscured, he passed through the gate and walked past the twelve-foot high wooden palisades erected to give the village the appearance of a fort. Inside the open gates stood a black cannon and a pyramid of cannonballs. The bustling village lay before him; children cried out and women soothed them. He heard the clang of the smith's hammer and walked on.

Inside the thatched cottages of the English settlers, breezes stirred the drying herbs hung overhead and cooled the brows of the women, who never rested before the sun set. Wives and mothers swept away dust or carried wood inside for the supper's fire. Daughters churned butter and swatted at flies, softly humming hymns. Others hoed the gardens that provided the bulk of the simple fare they lived on, for tobacco was a cash crop that had to be weeded, wormed, and suckered but could not be eaten. There were animals to tend: free-roaming pigs and lowing cows, goats and chickens. If they died, families went hungry. Women and their older sons and daughters tended to the domesticated beasts. Washing and mending clothes was an unending task.

Passing the Powell cottage, Thomas set down the bucket to brush at the hair in his eyes and catch his breath. From just inside the shadowy doorway, doe-eyed Priscilla Powell looked boldly at Thomas and smiled, but said nothing; she held a broom in her hands as if she might take flight with it. Her mother, a widow, was a stern, solitary woman said to have the power to cast spells for good and evil. Holding two live chickens in her hands, the widow stared at Thomas for an uncomfortably long time. She had come to the doorway to see who was passing at midday. She was short and squat, with dark eyes hidden by dung-colored bangs. The widow never smiled and wasn't a happy person, even when her husband, who was a carpenter, had lived. She glared at Thomas as if she wished him turned into a toad.

Thomas saw a ladder against the chimney and thought to ask if he could help, but the widow always declined assistance. She was solitary by nature and distrustful of men and boys. The widow called out sharply to Priscilla, who dropped the broom and held the ladder as her mother climbed one rung after another, the chickens cackling and fluttering in her hands. As Thomas watched, the widow reached the top rung of the ladder and peering into the smokeless chimney, dropped the chickens in, as if feeding them to a black mouth. The squawking was terrible. In a moment, the soot-covered birds emerged in the doorway, the widow scuttled down the ladder, and the Powell chimney was clean.

Thomas shook his head in wonder at the widow's ways. Up the street a dog barked, then howled like a wolf, a bad sign. His blood ran cold, and a shiver ran up his spine.

Thomas hurried on, complaining inwardly. The weight

of the bucket threatened to pull his shoulders out of their sockets. Surely the berries weighed as much as a hogshead barrel of tobacco: half a ton! His hands burned, and every twenty paces or so, he set down the bucket, expecting his palms to burst into flames. Thomas felt the widow Powell's eyes burn into his back with a flame so real he was tempted to turn around and plead with her not to set him ablaze. Less kind folks whispered that the widow withered crops and caused chickens to stop eating and die, but Thomas's mother scoffed at such nonsense, and his father would have no idle gossip spoken within his house.

He walked farther on the broad dusty path, past the spacious cobblestone and timber church, the company storehouse, the grand two-chambered Houlgrave house built of native brick and stone, John Read's open-air smithy, and the modest Laydon home and soon came to his family's one-room cottage. There was no smoke coming from the chimney; supper would be cold tonight, perhaps apples, cheese, and bread.

From habit, he glanced at the crude wooden cross planted in the earth near the fenced-in vegetable plot, marking where his infant brother lay buried, dead before he even drew a breath. The zigzag split rail fence needed repair or the hogs would be back to eat more of their corn and squash. Thomas dropped the bucket to pull a weed from the grave. Around the perimeter of the garden, his mother had planted flowers that reminded her of home, of England: primroses and tulips, daffodils and daisies. They bloomed hastily in the Virginia sunshine and collapsed in the midday heat, like a good many people unaccustomed to the climate. Chickens squabbled and fought for kernels of corn in the thatch and wood barn, which was not much more than a lean-to with no door; inside, the lone cow lowed. She must be hungry, Thomas thought. A barrel of corn stalks, winter feed, stood empty in the shadows of the far corner. I wonder if she'd eat a strawberry? For fun, he tossed one into the shadows within the small outbuilding. With a quick prayer for the everlasting peace of his little brother's soul, Thomas lifted the bucket one last time.

Pleased with himself, he set the bucket in the dirt just

outside the open doorway with a thump that would surely raise his mother from her bed. He blew on his palms to soothe them and waited to hear his mother's step inside the thatched cabin. Won't she be pleased with me, he thought. The Indian salve had all but disappeared and his hands no longer ached. The burning and itching relented too, as if by magic. Thomas knew what Wotton the surgeon meant when he said the savages use medicines never dreamed of by Englishmen. In Thomas's experience, the surgeon bled those who needed it and gave snake oil to others. Sometimes he just shook his head. Thomas's father said a surgeon's profession was the only one in which a man buried his mistakes.

"Berries for all!" Thomas called out. He listened. Nothing. The welt in his forehead throbbed. His lips stuck together, he was so in need a drink. He ladled water to his lips from the bucket by the doorway and drank deeply, spilling some and not caring. If his mother had seen, she would have scolded him for wasting even a drop. It was a long walk to the river, and the village well was brackish in the summer. Those who drank from it suffered ague and fevers which left them weak and ill-spirited. So many women had died in the two years that Thomas and his family had lived in Jamestown that he could no longer name them all, although his mother could, when her memory served her and the fevers let her be.

The strawberries begged to be eaten. Had he not endured an Indian attack to keep hold of them? Smiling at his own jest, he sat and ate one pimpled berry after another, brushing the dirt off with his sleeve. The forbidden fruit of the tree in the Garden of Eden could not have tasted half as pleasing, Thomas decided. He burped, pardoned himself, and laughed aloud. Where was Mother, who was usually so quick to scold him for poor manners?

With the men and their servants off in the tobacco fields pruning and watering the precious gold leaf, Thomas was surprised to see Jack of the Feathers shuffling down the dusty way in the midday heat. The sinewy heathen carried a musket in one hand and sported a feather cloak; thus, his name. Like all Indians, Jack went by several names and seemed not to mind what the English called him. He came and went as he pleased, trading beads, ale, and axes to the Algonkians (his native people) for corn and squash. He occasionally worked in the tobacco fields himself for a trinket or a hatchet, but was notorious for being lazy and thieving every chance he got. Thomas knew enough to keep an eye on him. From what he had learned, none of the savages believed theft to be a sin; stealing something was a game to them, like kingpins. If they stole an axe from you, they expected you to try to steal it back. When the Governor ordered a thief's hand chopped off at the wrist, the thieving slowed but it never stopped. All Englishmen believed the natives to be heathens. Only Pocahontas, who died in England four years ago, gave her heart to God and was rewarded with a Christian name and a meeting with the King and Queen. Thomas's mother said that God so appreciated her conversion that he brought her up to Heaven at the first opportunity, when she was only twenty-two. Several local chiefs gratefully accepted the cross, as they would any trinket, but continued to worship false idols. The Jamestown minister all but gave up on converting them, as had most of the colony.

Jack of the Feathers knew some English and spoke it clearly, although verbs eluded him. Many a planter had learned a mouthful of Indian words from Jack, and trading between the two peoples grew more common, with both sides pleased if a little uneasy. The Indian wore trousers and sometimes a shirt, although this midday sun found him bare to the waist. Thomas wondered what errand Master Morgan had sent Jack on so early in the afternoon, when the men rested in the shade of the trees and drank liberally of the punch brought over from England by ship just a month before. Perhaps carrying the musket to his master (who relished nothing more than roast turkey breast), Jack cast a morose face and sauntered off with Thomas squatting on his haunches, watching him go. Jack moved with the lightfooted grace of a deer.

Thomas stood and wiped away the sweet strawberry juice from his lips and chin and entered the cottage. Something smelled rotten—probably the wild pears left too long in a bowl on the kitchen table. The fire in the stone hearth was out. He noticed that first. Usually he was taken by a coughing fit when he entered the cottage, for the fireplace leaked terribly, and Thomas's father was much too proud to seek help in patching it. So they coughed and suffered and rubbed their eyes, comparing the smoke to a London fog. But not today.

In the far corner stood the cupboard his father had made to store their utensils. On the table was the flour for bread, left uncovered. Flies buzzed around the lip of the honey bowl; Thomas shooed them, then noticed his mother as she lay still in her bed. On the floor by her side lay the damp cloth she used to cool her forehead. Her arm was outstretched.

Thomas took three steps toward his mother and collapsed in the folds of her apron, the heat of the fever that had slain so many maidens and mothers rising from her. The sobs and moans arising from within him almost terrified Thomas himself, they were so base; he sounded like a wolf with its foot caught in the iron jaws of a trap. He wept with no concern for place or propriety, calling her name over and over, pleading with God to undo this wrong. Why would the Good Lord who brought them here two years ago allow her to perish now? They had endured ten weeks at sea, living like Jonah in the belly of the whale, battling storms and pestilence, famine and fever; now she lay dead. It made no sense to Thomas, so he wept and cried out for mercy.

Thomas had heard no one coming and jumped at the touch of someone gently enfolding him in her arms. He smelled the yeasty cotton apron of his mother and felt its cool, smooth fabric on his cheeks.

"Poor boy," his mother whispered, her voice a distant lullaby, "poor little man. You haven't lost me." A shudder ran through her, and Thomas held her so close she complained, "I cannot breathe, son." Her hazel eyes were clouded, or was it too dark in the cottage to see their brightness clearly? She pulled at the collar around her neck as though it were choking her.

As he wiped away his tears, his mother closed her eyes

and shivered, pulling him close. "It's cold and dark."

Thomas wanted to tell her about the berries and hot June sun. He spoke up. "I'll make a fire!" He tried to pull free of her grasp to begin the task but could not.

"No. Find Mrs. Garret. Go." Her voice was weak.

Thomas raced out the doorway and down the dusty street to Matthew's house. Mrs. Garret met him in the doorway, the sun slanting in to fall like a beam upon their table, two long boards laid across empty barrels. She listened for a moment, hushed him, and grabbed a leather pouch from a peg inside the door.

Mrs. Garret's herbs and care brought his mother to her feet before supper, when the men returned from the tobacco fields and the sun passed to the west, illuminating the mountains, and some believed, the vast blue water of the ocean that lay hidden just beyond. Thomas longed to see for himself what lay a hundred miles to the west, but his father dismissed the notion as madness and a waste of precious energy. He had crossed ocean enough to get to Virginia.

His father entered their home with a quiet dignity Thomas envied. A tall, lean, and tight-lipped man, he had left England a poor farmer and come to Virginia to grow fifty acres of tobacco and to get rich fast. He had been seasick for much of the sailing and had no appetite for adventure. Uneducated, he was wise enough to know that coming to Virginia was a once-in-a-lifetime opportunity to own land and to make money, so he came, bringing along his family. They came with the promise of land and livestock and tools. This much he had told Thomas at bedtime, when the boy begged for a story, but his father would say little about their family left behind in England.

Thomas remembered England too. He went to bed hungry back home. His mother wept a good deal. They were sick in the winter and never had more than five shillings in the tin. Every day it rained, and in the winter, sleet hissed in the fire and stung him as he did his chores outside. Thomas was promised books and schooling but never got them. He too had little stomach to cross the Atlantic Ocean again and return to England. This was their home now, and here they would claim their fortune — or lose everything trying.

This evening, Charles Spencer greeted his wife and son by name, washed the dirt from his face and hands at the bucket by the door, and sat at the table, tearing off a piece of bread for himself. The fireplace spewed smoke: a grey cloud hung over the candle and inhabited their clothes and hair. Their eyes stung.

"One day, I'll patch that fireplace," his father said. His mother cast a doubting glance at her husband.

Thomas's mother then spoke up, scolding him. She reminded him to say grace, a prayer he so hurried through that he was forced to repeat it. Thomas asked his father about what lay to the west and if any men spoke of traveling there. Might the two of them join such a party one day and see land no Englishmen had ever set foot on before? Perhaps they would find the fabled Back Sea to China!

"We are here to grow tobacco and to civilize the land and the heathens, son," explained his father. "Savages do not eat at a table nor live in a cottage nor worship the one true God. Men who lust after gold fare little better." The lines in his forehead seemed to grow deeper each day he spent in the fields. He looked to be much older than thirty-five, Thomas thought, but so did all the men of Jamestown, except the Reverend, who did no work and rarely went out in the daylight. "That is our mission. All this talk of gold in the mountains and the Sea of China is a sin. God has blessed our journey here and provided for us. We have girdled and felled the trees and tamed the wilderness. Let us give thanks and let temptation pass us by unfettered. Amen."

They supped on stew cooked in a long-handled skillet they had brought with them from England. Thomas said nothing of his mother's illness, nor did she.

Raising the spoon to his mouth, his father paused. Thomas felt the blood rise in his face. "What's happened to your head, boy? Looks like you kissed a woodpecker and she kissed back."

"Charles, such talk!" his mother said. Her eyes were bright with amusement. "The boy is supping."

Thomas did not want to lie. His mother had pretended

not to notice the swelling on his forehead, so Thomas had prepared no story and was unrehearsed. "I bumped it."

"On what? The stew is good, Mary." His father always ate everything on his plate, ate more than Thomas ever could, yet he grew leaner by the day.

Thomas looked to his mother for help, but she kept her eyes downcast, as if the vegetables and broth she stared into were of endless fascination. Thomas was on his own now. The fire popped and crackled. A rooster crowed. "I picked a bucketful of strawberries—"

"I saw them," his father said. "You almost filled the bucket." He emptied the water in his flagon. His mother stood to refill it. "Is that what that knot on your head is, a berry pushing to get out?"

Thomas never knew when to laugh at his father's jests. It seemed that when he did, his father scolded him for seeming foolish, and if he did not, his mother urged him to stop being so gloomy. So he smiled dumbly, like a cow, and kept his silence.

His father took another long drink, then set down the flagon and looked right into Thomas's eyes. "Explain yourself, son. Tell me a tale of your own devising."

Thomas thought to begin, "Once upon a time ..." But his parents had little tolerance for high-spirited children. Smoke from the fire burned his eyes. Why must there always be a fire, even in the inferno of summer? He smelled the sour odor of fear all about himself. Surely his father did also. "I wrestled an Indian boy. He took some of my berries."

"Did he strike you?" his father asked. He leaned close, folding his hands into a cathedral. His eyes blazed with anger, Thomas thought.

"No, sir. We wrestled. It was all play to him. I got poked and we went to the river and put mud on it and I saw Indians fishing and he made a sign—"

"Whoah! Whoah, boy! What about the knot?" His father leaned back now, reassured that his son was not the target of a savage attack.

"He hit me in the head with an unripe berry. I took it as a heathen greeting."

After a pause when he seemed frozen in surprise, his father threw back his head and laughed as loud and hard as Thomas had ever heard him. Even his mother smiled, showing her fine teeth, a girl's pretty white teeth. Thomas had to laugh. He rubbed the swelling and his father laughed all the more.

"How does he say goodbye, knocking you on the head with his tomahawk?" his father joked. Then he grew serious; Thomas dreaded the coming advice. Another freedom lost—he should have kept his mouth shut or lied. "You'd best stay out of the woods alone, son, or you'll come home unrecognizable. Only an Indian maiden will wed you, you'll be so ugly. Let's eat the berries Thomas risked his life for, Mary."

Thomas exhaled in relief. He was free to wander. A miracle! As his mother stood to clear the table and wash the plates, she seemed to stagger. Thomas did not know what to do and sat there as his father stood and ran to hold her up.

"Lie abed, Mary; the boy will serve us."

Thomas ran out back to fetch the cream from the cold house. A breeze stirred in the treetops but he could not feel it. The night would be hazy but at least there was no rain in sight. He said a silent prayer for his mother's health and dashed back in with the covered cream pitcher. They feasted until his father had to open his belt. By the rushlight, the room was no longer gloomy and dark and small as a cell; with a full belly, Thomas no longer feared the night and the deep woods so nearby.

That night, at bedtime, his father's hand seemed to linger on his shoulder, as if Thomas were about to receive a heavy-handed blessing. His father listened intently as Thomas prayed the Our Father, then arose to close the shutters. Gnats buzzed around Thomas's face; he brushed them from his eyes. He slept fitfully on the corn husk mattress, dreaming of England, but in his dream there was no hunger, and the sun shone on his mother's face, and her smile was blinding, like a beam of light shooting down from Heaven.

✦ ✦ ✦

Outside the church on Sabbath day, Thomas spied Matthew Garret practicing his best scowl. Had the boy nothing better to do? A crowd of husky lads pushed and shoved to stand near the oxlike fellow, who stood a head above the other boys his age. Matthew pulled at his collar; his bullneck strained at the white fabric. The boy was not made to wear Sunday collars. The sneer he cast at Thomas might have sent a bulldog whining to its pen.

From within the chapel, both bells rang the call to worship. Thomas took a deep breath, stayed close to his parents, and entered the church. Other families crowded inside the chapel too, where the air was close and the light dim in the morning haze. One of the finer gentlewomen waved a fan in her face. Her husband, a gentleman rich in land and money, wore gold lace on his coat and shiny leather boots. His russet-colored doublet fit snugly over his chest and shoulders. Thomas heard whispers of disapproval that such frippery did not belong in God's House, but he thought the clothes beautiful and planned to wear an outfit just like it when he returned from China with sacks of gold.

People stood shoulder to shoulder; the cedar pews were filled with worshippers. Broad windows were thrown open to allow light and air into the congregation; outside, a flock of pigeons flew over, thousands of them. Their cooing brought the congregation to silence. A planter standing next to Thomas looked up, no doubt wishing he were outside with his musket. Roast pigeon was a good dish, and when so many flew over, to shoot and miss was well nigh impossible. A man might bring down a half-dozen or more with one shot. Someone's stomach growled as if a beast inside were tortured beyond endurance.

Reverend Wilson cleared his throat and stepped past the black walnut communion table and paused at the cedar pulpit, a Bible in hand. At the Reverend's feet, the baptismal font lay empty, carved out of cedar and burned out like a small canoe. Reverend Wilson was a short, stocky man perpetually short of breath and red-faced, as if overexerted, yet he never did a lick of work, and some planters thought the less of him for it.

"Let us pray," the Reverend began, and they did, for what seemed an hour. "'While the earth remaineth, seed-time and harvest, and cold and heat, and summer and winter, and day and night shall not cease.' So says the Good Book, in Genesis, eight, twenty-two. The earth remaineth, does it not?" The Reverend cleared his throat and spoke further. "We bring Christianity to the heathen. We offer the savage Heaven for a small piece of this fallen earth. He must choose wisely and soon, for God has given us power and might far beyond his devils and his arrows and his tomahawks. We walk in the Lord's footsteps; so must he!"

Thomas was soon lost in the monotonous drone of the sermon, but understood it to have something to do with the mixing of the races, a sin against God expressly prohibited by the prophet Ezra, chapter ten, in the Old Testament. Thomas had heard of men, English planters and adventurers, who had turned their backs on civilization and taken to living with the savages upriver and inland, but he knew none of the men, and the stories seemed more like fables. What wicked magic did Powhatan's folk wield that so jumbled a man's natural sense and judgment? The very idea gave Thomas a chill, and he shivered. His mother noticed and looked at him with alarm in her eyes. Many children had died of the fever too, more than a few of Thomas's age. He smiled to reassure her, and she returned her focus to the minister, who seemed in danger of preaching through all the daylight hours, contrary to custom. When he fidgeted with his shirt sleeve and tugged at the collar of his shirt, his father took him once by the arm and squeezed. Thomas got the message and stood stock-still till the sermon ended and they were dismissed to go with God and sin no more, all of which seemed hopelessly optimistic to Thomas.

In the dusty street outside, Matthew Garret pushed his way through the crowd and bent down to hiss in Thomas's ear: "I'll see you Monday next, berry-girl! Tell your father to bring a bucket to catch your blood." His breath smelled of wild onions and almost made Thomas sick. What tragedy could he invent to excuse himself from accompanying his father eight days hence?

Outside the church, the sun still surprisingly high in the sky after what seemed a sermon bent on keeping them indoors for most of the Sabbath day, Thomas and his parents lingered to greet their neighbors and to search out new Comers. Perhaps one of them came from Norwich north of London and had news of home. Gambling on success in Virginia, his father had left two brothers and his mother in Norwich, but his heart was English, Thomas knew, and he carried within him the deep desire to know that all was well with his kin. His mother had a married sister in London, her only living relative. Thomas was amused and heartened by this ritual; it was the only time of the week his father spoke more than a few words to anyone outside the walls of their home. His mother said little but listened to every word spoken and seemed to search the faces of the new Comers for clues of their origin, as if someone from the great city of London would surely know her sister, Anne Bourne of Wallace Street. No one ever did.

As his parents weaved through the hubbub of the murmuring crowd, Priscilla Powell popped up in front of Thomas as if dropped there from the sky. He must have looked surprised, for she opened wide her mouth and raised her eyebrows to mimic him.

"You look like a goggle-eyed catfish, Thomas Spencer," she said to him. She spoke to Thomas in quick honeyed tones, as if she always knew a secret and were aching to tell it. Her smile made him dizzy. Her hair spilled from beneath the white cap she wore; it looked like spun gold to Thomas. She smelled of roses and lilacs.

"My mother says we will trade you medicines for firewood. Shall we?" Priscilla spoke too loud for comfort; surely his mother would hear her and scold him. Why must such a pretty maid be so bold? Her hazel eyes caught his and held Thomas in a spell; he suddenly burned. Part of him wanted to cast off his coat and shirt and run barechested as Jack of the Feathers through the streets of

Jamestown, proclaiming his adoration of the flaxen-haired Priscilla.

Thomas could not find words to express thoughts better left unexplored. "I ... I ..."

The Widow Powell appeared beside her handsome daughter, who was taller and weighed half as much, and hushed her. Priscilla whispered something in her mother's ear and looking at Thomas, burst into peals of laughter that drew every eye in the village. Over his shoulder, as Thomas was hustled away by his mother (whose grip was surprisingly strong when inspired by dread), he saw the raised fist of Matthew Garret shaken in his direction, and a glare cast at him that would curdle fresh milk in the batting of an eye.

🪶   🪶   🪶

The fevers and fluxes came and went, leaving his mother delirious and weak. One day she removed a cloth from her ear and found it spotted with blood. Her feet swelled to the size of ripe melons. She spoke childishly to her mother and sister, one dead and the other five thousand miles away in London, as if they were in the room. She begged for water but would not drink when Thomas brought it. Frightened, he hastened to soothe her brow with a cool cloth. When the fever broke, she got to her feet to make a fire and sent him outside. Thomas passed a long afternoon hoeing weeds in the garden, dropping to his knees to pull tough, twisting vines from his infant brother's grave. His mother came to the doorway every few minutes to cast a cold eye upon his efforts and find fault with him.

If I picked every weed in the New World, Thomas thought, my mother would plant one just to spite me. He labored in the hot sun until supper, a meal they ate in silence, for his father's thoughts were already cast upon the tobacco, the gold leaf that would make them rich or ruin them. There was no talking to his mother about Priscilla Powell, for her mother was scorned as a witch, and association with her daughter could do Thomas naught but harm. On such matters his mother was unyielding. Thomas would marry a gentleman's daughter or not at all. His heart was an animal to be tamed like a goat, his mother reminded him, not a wily fox to run wild and lead him where it would. She went abed early and tossed often while Thomas's father struggled with numbers in the accounts ledger, figuring the best and worst they might expect from October's tobacco harvest. His mouth was tight and grim, and he used his fingers to add and to subtract, as a child would.

Thomas did not speak of it, but once, while gathering firewood at the forest's edge, he saw a red fox leaping through the brush, darting this way and that. The fox paused before a stand of loblolly pines, sniffed the air twice and vanished. Without being aware of it, Thomas had held his breath as he watched. The fox was master of his surroundings; the English would do well to be half as confident. The bushy tail raised by the beast stood defiant as a flag in that moment before he vanished. In his heart, Thomas was no goat, and he ran with the fox in his dreams that night.

🦊 🦊 🦊

On Friday next, after his father had broken the night's fast and left for the fields just after sunrise, Thomas dashed from their house and ran down the street to the little parsonage by the church. He found the minister seated on a bench beside the brick and timber meetinghouse, reading from the Good Book.

"Reverend, please," Thomas began, "My mother would send word to her sister in England."

The minister sighed. His heavy-lidded eyes reminded Thomas of a lazy lizard sunning itself on a log. "Yes? What of it, boy?"

Thomas gave the man his aunt's name and street in London and repeated the message just as his mother had forced him to memorize it. "Can the letter be sent across the ocean to England on the next ship?" he asked, as his mother had instructed him.

The minister got to his feet with a heavy sigh. "It can— for fifty pounds of tobacco."

Thomas agreed. It seemed like a lot of tobacco for so few words, but his mother had admonished him not to argue with Reverend Wilson, who was a man of God in a land of heathens and sinners. Thomas wished again that he could read more than a few simple words and write more than his name, but his father knew little more of the language and his mother less. No one but the minister, a scrivener, the handful of landed gentlemen of Jamestown, and a few of the shippers read and wrote much more than he, so at least he bore no shame for his ignorance. Like his secret desire to see and to cross the blue mountains, he yearned to read the Old Testament for himself, to read the words of the prophets with his own eyes, and to learn the lessons of the book in privacy, without having to endure the unpleasant smugness of the minister, a man fat with knowledge but lean of heart.

The preacher led him inside to the bench that was his desk but had no sooner set pen upon paper when voices were raised, and an oath rarely heard in the streets of Jamestown arose.

"Men have been whipped for saying less!" the Reverend snapped. Enraged, he dropped the quill pen onto the table and tottered out the door. Thomas followed. Hens clucked and scattered before them.

A crowd of twelve citizens had gathered outside the widow Powell's house. Thomas felt a sharp pain in the pit of his stomach; the hysteria in their shrill voices struck him like a knife. A giant of a man unknown to him raised his fist at the widow Powell, who stood defiantly in her doorway, shaking a broom, shooing them from her property. The minister intervened, calling for a path to clear and let him through.

Thomas approached but stayed outside the ring of angry men and women, for he did not want Priscilla or her mother to think him one of them. The air was sharp with pitch, the natural tar of a nearby bog. A witch gave off just such an odor, as everyone knew.

The man called for the witch to be punished. His baritone voice rumbled like the Prophet Ezra's must have. "She withered my corn and choked my hens because I call her what she is! A witch! Witch!" A cloud of black flies suddenly swirled around the man's head; he swatted at them, but they would not depart. "She sent the flies to torment me!" he cried, ducking this way and that. "It's her doing!"

Others took up the cry. Reverend Wilson interposed himself between the man and the widow, who came forward boldly, walking up to them without fear. Thomas wished she might show even a glint of reticence. The preacher hushed the man who led the accusers, and for once Thomas raised a cheer within for the sawed-off minister. The Widow and the Reverend huddled close without touching, speaking softly, while the crowd called for her trial and punishment.

Thomas looked on with apprehension. His heart raced when Priscilla appeared around the corner of the mean house, an albino piglet in her arms. She hugged the animal, which squealed and kicked its stubby legs, but she would not let it go. Seeing Thomas, she kissed the pig on the mouth and smiled, holding up the creature for his inspection. Flustered, Thomas took a step back. No one else seemed to take notice of her. Priscilla laughed and spoke again to the pig. Such nonsense did her mother's cause no good, Thomas knew.

Frightened by the talk of punishing the widow Powell, Thomas ran home to tell his mother. She must do something. Regardless of his mother's feelings, she must not let a poor widow be punished as a witch—unless she was a witch. Reverend Wilson could be counted on to do what was right, Thomas knew, but sometimes what was right hurt a good deal. Fearing for Priscilla as well as her mother, he wished his father were home; he would know what to say, or at least stand up to the crowd with a well-chosen word or two should the minister withdraw. He ran too fast to be careful and stumbled. With horror, he looked down upon an abandoned grave. Thomas scrambled to his feet and jumped backwards over the mound of earth, erasing the curse. He hurried home.

Inside, on the raised platform bed three feet above the

dirt floor lay his mother. He watched so intently that he held his breath and dared not blink. He willed her to breathe. She did not move. Thomas took her hand, which felt like alabaster, smooth and cold to the touch. Yet her dead hand seemed to clutch his and squeeze, holding onto him, dragging him into that domain of no exit.

"Father! Father! Father!" Thomas called out until like his mother, he too had no breath. He heard footsteps in the dirt and tore free of her eternal grasp, she who had left him too soon and too far from home.

Chapter Two

EAGLE OWL'S DREAM

Eagle Owl pulled his dugout canoe out of the broad green river and onto the muddy banks choked by weeds and gnarled roots. The sweet stink of the shallow water welcomed him; longtailed gnats buzzed and bit. He should have been fishing, but he had to learn more about the new people. Surely his father would understand a young man's curiosity.

It was the berry season, when the women and children of Quiyoughcohannock passed long sunny days picking wild strawberries, plums, herbs, and tuckahoe roots. In this season, his younger sisters and brothers ate their fill and more and were never scolded. They ran naked through the woods looking for berries, nuts, and firewood; keeping the fire inside the yehawkin going was a child's task, night and day. Without the fire, the house would mildew and rot, and the deer flies and gnats would make many a meal of them all. Laughter trailed the children wherever they ran.

The shore mud was cool and massaged his bare feet. He dragged the canoe into the bushes and turned it over. The smoke of cooking fires rose in the sky, and the sharp scent of wood burning drew him home. He was hungry and ran down the narrow, twisting path toward the fish drying on the cooking coals.

Eagle Owl came upon a fallen wasps' nest by grace. It lay on the forest floor like a gift. From up high, a hawk's piercing cry erupted: what was its meaning? Eagle Owl looked up but the hawk was gone. Was the cry of the hawk a warning from Grey Hawk, his rival for Quiet Lark's love and affections? Why would the god reward him now if not to bless his meeting and befriending the young intruder, the boy with the sky-colored eyes? He bent down, took the nest in his hands, and carefully peeled away the papery layers from the many-chambered comb until the young white wasps appeared, unable to fly or sting but fully formed and alive. They were crunchy honey in his mouth, a delicacy to be treasured. He savored one more bite and suck, saved most of the nest, and ran toward the village with his heart full of pride: he had a gift to share, something special. His mother and father would be pleased. The children would wrestle for more, more!

He came to the springs and a small clearing and approached the palisades marking and protecting the village. Neat rows of corn and squash sent up green signs of the coming harvest. The gardens were in flower, and the corn stood two feet high. Women hoed weeds between the neat rows of corn, squash, pumpkins, and sunflowers. As Eagle Owl walked past the sprouting mounds, children and women greeted him. Naked boys and girls jingled little bells, gifts from the English, and hooted and flapped their arms to chase away crows, who squawked in reply and flew just a few feet before landing and turning around, hoping the guardians of the garden would tire and let them eat. The children were vigilant: chasing away the scavenging birds was as much a game as it was work, and their mothers and aunts and grandmothers praised them lavishly for keeping the blackbirds at bay. The green corn they grew now would feed them through the winter, no matter how cold or dark the deer and bear hunting season might be.

Inside the ring of felled tree trunks planted securely in the ground, twenty long houses stood in scattered clusters. Eagle Owl slipped between the wall of oaks marking the village boundaries; the gap was no more than a foot wide and would slow a Monacan or an intruder bent upon making trouble, though it would not stop him.

Cooking fires dotted the ground. Eagle Owl paused to watch the women potters, who mixed raw red clay with smashed, burned mussel shells. They shaped the clay and shells by hand, forming a pot or a dish or a jar as if by magic. Fascinated, their children watched, and learned. Using a mussel shell, the women smoothed the surface, polishing it with a rubbing stone. Eagle Owl trotted along his way. Where was Quiet Lark?

He saw her sitting in a circle of girls, with her smooth brown back to him, under the broad shade of an oak tree. She was bare to the waist, bent over, weaving a reed basket; her back was bent like a bow, taut and perfect. Eagle Owl had begun to dream of her, proof of his love for her and their entwined destiny. One day soon, after the huskanaw and her coming of age, he would offer her family fresh game, beads, furs, and skins, and they would wed. He had dreamt of the ceremony too, of the breaking of a bead necklace over their joined hands, of the flutes and drums and the people dancing in the firelight, and of the good-natured horseplay in the couple's first night together, as man and wife. The singing would go on through the night, frightening the whippoorwills and silencing the crickets, until the dawn, when exhausted and hoarse, the merry-makers fell asleep in their yehawkins. More than one fire would die that night, and in the morning, sleepy-eyed children would be scolded until the fire was made again. After that day, Eagle Owl would live with Quiet Lark in her home, and he would be a hunter, a warrior, and a provider. Only Grey Hawk challenged him, and he had little standing, being the third son of a hunter who was neither chief nor priest.

One of the other maidens touched Quiet Lark's arm, and thirty feet away, she turned shyly and glanced at him. Her dark hair fell into her eyes; she brushed it away gently, as if a hummingbird had lighted there and was frightened. Her cheekbones glistened, polished like a gemstone; in her eyes shone a light that cut Eagle Owl like a knife. She saw through his skin and flesh and into his heart, and she smiled. When she returned to her work, he heard the other girls giggling and questioning her, but she shook her head and said nothing. She could keep a silence too, he thought: how can I count all of her good traits?

Eagle Owl turned away, wondering where his mother

was. He ought to greet her first and see what kind of mood his father was in. Scattered groves of elm and sycamore trees stood between the arched, domelike houses where the people of Quiyoughcohannock lived. The houses were covered by large woven mats. They reminded Eagle Owl of the homes birds made in the trees, homes of wood and leaves, round and pliant as a honeybee's nest. Bent saplings supported the houses inside, their tips planted firmly in the packed, raised earth of the smooth, cool floor. The yehawkins had no windows but most bore two doors covered by reed mats, which were rolled up in the day to let in the air and the light. To Eagle Owl, the village was a welcoming circle of people, food, and shelter.

"Wingapo." Two of Little Dove's daughters ran to greet him. If he married Quiet Lark, Little Dove's eldest daughter, he would live with them. He glanced away for a moment and saw the boys practicing in the meadow, shooting arrows at bits of moss and sticks thrown into the air by older brothers. The boys would not eat until they hit a target. Little Dove's daughters were naked, as were all Powhatan children until puberty, and clung to Eagle Owl like a brother. They had been playing in the shallows of the river and were wet and glistening as otters, and just as playful. They warned him: "Your father is angry; you crossed the river for no good reason."

He broke off a small piece of the wasp nest for each of them and playfully shoved them away with his foot as they charged, chewing greedily and demanding more. Their laughter rose and fell over itself, like the chattering of squirrels darting between the oaks in search of acorns. Flat corn bread baked outside in pits covered by leaves and ashes. Game roasted on sticks suspended above the fires; pots rested in hot coals, cooking squash and beans. The smells tortured Eagle Owl; his stomach growled like a bear. The children laughed and teased him, calling him "Hungry Bear! Hungry Bear!"

Oholasc hushed them and beckoned to her son from the entrance to their house. She wore a deerskin breechcloth-apron and smelled of smoke and fish. A proud and strong woman, she was said to have the eyes of a cougar and could see as well at night as the big forest cat. Like the other married women, her hair was cropped to one length, just below the ears. With a needle made from bone, she mended a breechcloth torn in the woods. She seemed angry and offered her only son no smile or word of greeting.

Inside the oblong yehawkin, which stretched for thirty feet, Eagle Owl let the reed mat drop. The shade was welcome, but the smoke and heat of the fire annoyed the boy, who longed to dive in the river to cool off. Deer flies buzzed incessantly unless he stood in the smoke of the fire, which stung his eyes. The circle of rocks surrounding the central firepit was smooth and perfect; from overhead, sunlight entered the house through the hole in the ceiling. A fishing net hung from the ceiling, waiting to be repaired. It seemed to accuse him of slothfulness. A scaffold of reeds covered with mats reached almost to the ceiling; in the loft, corn and fish dried — more food for the winter. Firewood was piled under the sleeping benches, raised wooden platforms covered with hides and furs that spilled onto the hard dirt floor. Corn filled the reed baskets stacked inside the yehawkin, the long house where everyone Eagle Owl loved slept, all save his father, where a fire always burned and the rain never dared to enter. Chestnuts, walnuts, hickory nuts, and boiled acorns would soon fill other large baskets. Clubs and bows rested just inside the door, where men could grab them quickly. Pots and baskets holding corn stood against the far wall of the house, food to be held in reserve for emergencies, food that too often went to the intruders to buy peace and to stave off their foolish starvations. Ceremonial eagle feathers lay drying, held upside down on a rawhide string. Eagle Owl noticed his bow, quiver of arrows, and leather wrist and arm guards placed just inside the door, where he always put them. The leggings he wore in the deep woods lay beside the bow and the long fishing spear. His reed flute and tobacco pipe stood against the wall. Music and smoke, Eagle Owl thought, his father's great passions — but for the hunt. Would he inherit the same desires and a similar wisdom and physical courage? He prayed to the gods to be half as brave and wise as his father, Great Eagle.

His mother offered her son blackened, roasted fish which crumbled in his hands. She asked nothing, but the boy knew he must explain his absence soon.

"The fire is almost out," he teased. His mother did not laugh. It was bad luck to let a fire go out. Dry leaves and moss lay outside the ring of stones within which the fire burned. With the moss and tinder and a rounded wooden friction stick, his mother could make a fire in moments, if the children neglected it in the night.

"Eagle Owl!" his father called from outside. His voice was deep and sharp.

His mother turned her head. He set down the fish and emerged from the long house, following his father through the village and toward the river, keeping a distance of respect and fear, uncertain of his father's tone or intent. They passed the larger yehawkin where his father lived. As werowance, he lived alone and would do so until he wed again and had another child. Then, his second wife and child would move to a home of their own.

Great Eagle motioned for his son to follow and led him to the banks of the great river, where he folded his arms and stood silent, waiting. He was a tall, muscular man who wore a fringed breechcloth. Around his neck were strung four bead necklaces. The turkey feather that jutted from the crown of his head swayed in a soft, warm breeze that brought with it the decay of the sea and the deep mushroomy odor of mud. Eagle Owl looked up at his father, wondering if he would ever grow so straight and tall, and if the men would listen to him as he spoke.

Ten feet inland from the river, two men making a canoe burned a cavity into a log twenty feet long; smoke rose curling and wispy into the canopy of trees, giving off a sweet scent, the smell of work and promise. The smoke drifted across the river in high wispy clouds before disappearing in the river's hazy light. As one man fanned the fire with a reed fan, the other scraped at the burned wood with the sharp edge of a shell, patiently forming the dugout.

Eagle Owl grew impatient; he was hungry and weary and wanted to give away the rest of his forest gift and to feast on berries. Why had his mother, who should listen to

his tale of the blue-eyed intruder without interrupting or
scolding him, sent him off to swat flies and to sweat in the
drenching heat, waiting for his father to speak?

"Where are the fish you have caught?" his father asked.
"Grey Hawk has brought a basket of oysters and eels for
his family." The muscles in his forearms jumped whenever
he moved his hands. Eagle Owl was reminded of his father's great strength in every movement the werowance
made. "Are you named poorly? Should you be called Silent
Owl?"

The boy looked away; his father must have guessed
that he had crossed the river and had no fish or game to
show for his efforts. "I brought young wasps in the nest.
Sweet as honey. A reward from the gods, don't you think,
father?" He showed his father the nest. He then broke off a
piece and offered it to Great Eagle, who took it slowly and
raised it to his lips as if it might fly away buzzing to the
moon. He chewed and savored the sweetness just as the
children had.

His father pointed across the broad waters of the river.
The far shore was covered in a haze, and the trees appeared to be very small. "Our people across the river live
with the intruders like brothers; we are not brothers. Okewas has shown them to be our enemies. They take land as
if we handed it to them. They take our corn by force yet
plant only tobacco, which no man can eat. The intruders
make no sense."

Eagle Owl had to speak; his throat was dry, yet he
dared not run to the river to drink, not before he spoke. "I
came upon one of them, a young man my age, but lean as a
buck in winter. We wrestled and I hurt him."

"What was he doing?" His father's voice was deep and
flat, interested but hiding the curiosity.

"Picking berries."

Great Eagle looked his son in the eyes. The chieftain's
forehead wrinkled in concern. "Was he lame?"

Eagle Owl replied that he was not. Great Eagle was
puzzled; why was the boy not fishing or setting traps or
hunting wild turkey to feed his family?

His father reminded Eagle Owl of the diseases and

droughts of the last few years, and skirmishes with the intruders that left two of their hunters dead. "The intruders suffer also. They will leave, never to return. Or we must force them to go."

Eagle Owl wished that were not so but said nothing. His father was a werowance and need listen to no one but the priest, who cast spells and saw the future in dreams and visions. Nothing was guaranteed him but food and a place by the fire.

His father broke Eagle Owl's reverie with a stern reminder of his duty to the village and his family. "When you come back, bring fish." He dismissed his son with a slow, elegant wave of his hand. The work on the canoe continued, the scraping of the blade making eerie music in the haze of the afternoon.

Eagle Owl outran the biting flies and dashed back to his mother's fire to gorge himself on blackened, dried fish, green corn, and a nibble of the crispy wasp hive. He licked his fingers dry and ran for water, the smaller children in pursuit, shaking gourds filled with seeds and beating hide drums, eager to hear of his beating by his father. They did not believe Eagle Owl when he told them that he was not beaten and seemed genuinely disappointed, so he tossed stones at them to chase them back to work and off to play in the fields. He quickly told his mother the story of the English boy and ran off toward the temple before she could scold him; the priest would understand.

Grey Hawk dropped in front of him from the sky. Eagle Owl gasped and froze, adding to his rival's merriment. Grey Hawk was as old as the werowance's son, fifteen autumns, but broader and faster, and as good a hunter as any man. He had a sharp nose and the broad round head of a thinker. Many said that he would surely be the next werowance, for his father was a good hunter and provided for two wives and many people. It was like him to drop from a ten foot high branch of an elm tree and risk injury just to frighten Eagle Owl.

Grey Hawk opened wide his mouth before speaking, mocking Eagle Owl's surprise. "You frighten like an old woman," he said, sneering.

"You drop from a tree like bird dung," Eagle Owl replied, "which I also avoid." He tried to slip by but the bigger boy blocked his path.

"What do you do across the river, with the intruders? Do you court their girls or serve their fathers like a slave?" Grey Hawk tensed, expecting a fight.

Eagle Owl breathed deeply through his nose, a calming breath his father had taught him. He held his ground and smelled the smoke and sweat and fishy stink of his rival, who ground his teeth, he was so eager to fight. Unless Eagle Owl struck first, Grey Hawk would be blamed for starting the fight with no good cause, and he would lose standing as a leader. Eagle Owl looked him in the eye. "I serve our people there, as here."

Grey Hawk snorted. "As a scout? Who sent you, the dead werowance Powhatan? What do you do that is so much a secret that your own father must ask you to explain?" He grasped his hands and pulled up with both arms, reaching for the sky, and a sharp crack of his bones proclaimed his readiness to wrestle.

Eagle Owl had heard enough. He owed no words of explanation to Grey Hawk or any other save his father and the priest. "Go and bathe in the river, or you will be called Three Days Dead Hawk."

Grey Hawk was so surprised by the words that he stood tensed but unmoving as Eagle Owl walked past him, bumping him at the shoulders. Grey Hawk spun and coiled, but his rival walked on as if he had not noticed the contact. Grey Hawk jumped into the air and smashed the earth with his bare feet, he was so angry. He howled and cursed and tore a sapling from the earth, casting it roots and all ten feet into the air. When would the boy fight him? When could he grind his heel into Eagle Owl's neck and show Quiet Lark she had chosen a weak suitor and a coward? When?

Eagle Owl found Namontack the priest sitting inside the quioccosan—the temple—oiling the small lock of hair on the right side of his head, which all other Powhatan men shaved clean. Over the fire, pokeberry leaf tea brewed; it smelled terrible but cured smallpox, which had ravaged the children of the village. In the corner lay small covered bowls of snakeroot and willows, which ended fevers, and pinkroot to worm a child who might otherwise die. Namontack's medicines were powerful; he was a healer of great repute, and in his presence, Eagle Owl knew enough to be quiet.

The priest wore a deerskin mantle; he did not greet the chief's son but seemed to know the boy was there, ready to help. Without waiting to be told, Eagle Owl carefully laid more firewood upon the flames burning just outside the open-air wall of the building, facing the rising sun.

A breeze blew through the temple. Resting in neat lines on the elevated loft were the dead werowances of the past fifty years, their pale naked corpses touching only at the shoulder. Guarding them was the grotesque scorched image of the black-faced god of evil, Okewas, crouched and ready to spring at the enemies of the people who dared to disturb the rest of these great men. Eagle Owl prayed that one day his father would lie here, and his heart beat faster with pride, and he was no longer hot and tired.

He added wood to the fire until it roared and the old priest raised his hand: Enough! The priest sat amongst piles of skins, tribute to the werowance and to the priest from their grateful people. Corn rested in heaping baskets in the far corner of the temple, near smaller reed containers of copper, a rare and valuable metal, and shell beads, a symbol of a man's importance and things of beauty.

He approached the old priest, the quiyoughcosuck, whose face was wrinkled and whose eyes were slow to blink, like a turtle's. The old man lighted his pipe, inhaling the sharp, bitter tobacco and expelling smoke through his nose in two coiling streams, like clouds. Once he told Eagle Owl and his friends that the future could be seen in smoke, but they never knew when he was teasing them. His eyes were bloodshot, the whites streaked with red lines, as if the man never slept. Some said he was older than Powhatan, perhaps immortal. Eagle Owl hoped that today the priest would tell him something or ask a favor of him. Yet he knew that until the huskanaw and his coming into manhood, he could not be taught or shown the secrets of healing herbs and dreams that foretold a coming drought or the fate of the intruders.

The old man crooked a brown, cracked finger; Eagle Owl raced to his side. "Go away, squirrel," he said slowly, mouthing each word as if to devour it for sustenance. "Find a giant wasps' nest and feed all the people, if you can. Then I will hear your tales."

Stung by the priest's dismissal, Eagle Owl slunk away and returned to his home to eat and rest. How did the old man know of his surprise?

The sun had sunk below the crest of the tall oaks. A breeze from the river ruffled the feathers hanging inside the yehawkin. With the children outside yelping like pups, he found a cool dark place to lie down on the deerskins in the far corner and fell fast asleep.

🔻 🔻 🔻

He stands on the banks of the great river, which murmurs its song but lies hidden in a blanket of fog. (Why is the river hiding from me, he wonders.) He wills it so, and his arms (with a power of their own) extend his grasp to the top of the tallest oak and higher, until his fingers touch the clouds and squeeze the rain from them. He feels no pain and has little sense of wonder. The raindrops are cool and tap his forehead with a rhythm he finds pleasing. With his eyes closed, he feels for the far shores of the river; the banks are dry. Without saying a word, he nods to his people, and they begin to walk across the broad brown river from their village, stepping solemnly and without chatter to the western shore where the intruders await them. The English captain bows and greets Great Eagle, who offers him an eagle feather and a pipe. The Englishman smiles; his teeth are white as pearls. The Englishman waves, and all the English follow him across the river. Men, women with babes in their arms, children tall and squat—they all step lightly, walking upon Eagle Owl's outstretched arms as if they were a bridge of the finest timber. Their touch tickles him, and when he laughs, the people whoop with pleasure and surprise.

The people pass each other going both ways—east to west and sunset to sunrise. Men stand aside to let the women and children pass, and while there is no talk, the men are at ease with each other and smile. The people walking across his arms like ants tickle him, and he laughs again, a silent chuckle only the gods can share in, for the moment is perfect: he was born for just this moment.

* * *

Eagle Owl awakened with a start, his hand clawing the dirt. His mother stood over him, sprinkling his brow with drops of water.

"You have a fever," she said. "You were thrashing like a wounded stag."

He pushed aside the offered water and ran out of the house and into the night. Stars hung overhead, shimmering in the night mist, and the brutish song of the bullfrogs was incessant. A whippoorwill cried, the four notes a poor impression of a would-be owl demanding to know "Who?" He ran to the temple to awaken the priest, who slapped his hand away and muttered oaths that chilled the boy's blood. But he was persistent, and at last the old man sat up and asked, "What?"

Eagle Owl told the old priest his dream, the vision of himself as a human arch between the two peoples, a living, breathing, natural bridge over the river that divided the Algonkians and the English. The priest cut him off by clamping his tobacco-stained hand over the boy's mouth. He could barely breathe.

"I have heard enough. This is nonsense. Sleep now. Forget the dream. Do not speak of it again."

Eagle Owl spoke further. "It must be a vision! I have never dreamed a dream like this, never!"

"Go now or I'll banish you until your head clears, squirrel. Go!" The priest rolled on his side and settled back onto his reed mat and snored so loud that the who-ing whippoorwill flew away.

In his yehawkin, his mother sat waiting for him, stirring the coals in the soft fire burning in the center of the dirt floor. Taking a deep breath, he told her the dream, told her that it must be true and the old priest was lying or just too weary to weigh the truth, but she hushed him, offering him only water. He batted away the water and ran out into the darkness, racing past the fires burning low and through a break in the palisades toward the woods and the river, to his canoe and the cool freedom of the wind and the water, across to the other side, where the truth of his vision must be realized or he would die a fool.

An owl soared past him, scouring the banks of the river for a mouse, and asked again, "Who?" Eagle Owl thought, "Me, that is who," but he said nothing. The soft whish of the oar in the water soothed his anger. The night was his, the river was his alone. And the dream was his as well. Only his ...

Chapter Three

THE WRESTLING MATCH

His mother's funeral was held on Saturday. Thomas endured the ceremony, fighting back tears and heartache, biting his lip so fiercely that it bled, his hand clutched in his father's powerful grip. A few families had come from upriver, from both sides of the James, to attend the funeral. Few knew Thomas and his father except by name, for the Spencers were neither wealthy nor influential. Outside the church, there was no fusillade after the preacher's kind words over the coffin and a brief scripture reading; muskets were fired after a man died, and rum or cider was brought forth. The death of a woman, on the other hand, was a somber and speedy affair, for the women were precious and few, and far too many had died already.

Dressed in black cloth and with eyes downcast, the widow Powell and her daughter Priscilla stood respectfully in the rear of the crowd and were silent and downcast during the early part of the service; Thomas gave thanks for that. His mother's sudden death put an end to talk of witchcraft, at least for the while. That much good had come from his mother's passing. Later, he was mildly disturbed by the widow's whispered asides but understood nothing of what she said. Others seemed perturbed, and a few men openly hushed her, one man threatening to take her outside and thrash her. The Reverend silenced such idle chatter with a word about sins of commission and reminded the congregation (eyeing the widow Powell) that prayer was best undertaken in silence, behind closed doors, as "our Lord and Savior has taught us in the New Testament."

When the Reverend bowed his head, an uneasy silence reigned in the church. Even the cows and pigs were quiet for a moment, and the cries of the English sparrows nesting high in the ceiling halted. His father's hand, which was so hard from field work that it seemed carved of a block of wood, fell from his grasp with ease and finality. They were alone, together, a man and a boy, each lacking a woman, the same woman. Thomas could only imagine his father's pain and fear, solely because of his own. Was it more difficult losing a mother than a wife? Who but God could judge such a contest of woe? They were lost, the two of them, and they knew it. Thomas feared that if one small part of their lives changed—if a stew burned or Priscilla embraced him in the moonlight—they would both surely die. What foolish thoughts! Still, they haunted him and would not let him be.

The casket was carried to the Spencers' small plot of land. Thomas, his father, and four other planters held the rods that supported the wooden casket. How odd that his mother lay inside. She had breathed and laughed and scolded him just hours ago it seemed, and now she was in Heaven, free of pain and sacrifice and all earthly bonds. If only he could see her once more! To kiss her cheek, to hold her, to feel her cool hand on his fevered brow!

Sweat rolled down his face and tickled his neck. He felt dizzy, as if the earth were spinning and he but a tick clinging to it. The sharp stink of cow dung hit him in the nose, and he felt betrayed. Why had God made Man and Woman half-angel and half-beast?

They came to the hole in the ground which was to be his mother's new home forever. He glanced at Priscilla from the side of his eye and saw her covering her mouth, as if something wicked were gagging her. The widow had gone. Tears ran down the girl's rosy cheeks, and she made no move to dry them; Thomas was drawn to her for that small excess of grief. Priscilla barely knew his mother, yet she wept openly for her. Standing beside the dappled trunk of a peeling sycamore tree, the Powell girl slipped into Thomas's heart like the most secret adult wish, a dream of power and success and wealth, a desire the Reverend would squelch as evil and his father would mock as folly.

So be it; he loved the girl. She was beautiful and kind, and very alive. She grieved, she breathed, she was perfect in sorrow.

It seemed weird and wrong to lower his mother into the broken red earth as if she were a worm who might thrive there. His mother was an airy creature, weak of flesh but firm in spirit and a lover of light. She detested darkness and dreaded the long sea voyage in the dark hold of the ship where they huddled together for weeks, ill and hungry. When they landed at Jamestown, was she not the first to offer a prayer of thanks? Thomas fought back the tears that blinded him as they lowered the casket into the ground. The Reverend intoned, "Ashes to ashes, dust to dust," but Thomas heard no more. His ears were filled with screams, shouts of protest and agony that only after a period of quiet thought came to him as his own protests, in a deep man's voice as yet not granted him in the earthly domain. He shut his eyes and clenched his fists and waited for death's cold claw to reach for his throat, yet it did not come. The sun burned down on his bare head, the cow in the barn lowed stupidly, and in the sky high above them a lonesome hawk cried, taunting Thomas to do something. He could not move. His knees shook, and he was suddenly cold, as if winter had struck him alone with all its fury and ice.

Now Thomas's little brother had company, he thought; his mother's freshly-dug grave seemed a dark and dirty mistake. He waited for her to appear under the shade of the chestnut tree, wiping away a strand of hair that fell in her eyes, the hint of a smile playing across her face. How could the light that danced in her eyes be extinguished forever in an instant? Thomas could not fathom the irreversible nature of death.

Thomas glanced at his father. He wore his best white hose and shoes. His father believed in form and tradition; other men obeyed the law, his father trusted it. The long-sleeved white shirt hid the muscles in his arms, and under the broad brim of the worn felt hat his eyes were barely visible. Thomas detected a tremble in his father's lips and a facial tic. Longtailed gnats buzzed in their faces, and most men swatted at them vigorously, as if killing them were sport. His father seemed not to notice as a fly danced across his cheek.

His mother now lay under the living earth drained of blood, color, and desire. He was supposed to be pleased, said the Reverend. She had gone on to face God and to live in Heaven, a land of peace denied the heathens and unbelievers of all sorts. She would never again be hungry nor fear anything. Yet Thomas needed her touch on his face more than anything else, he had to hear her voice even in scolding, he must feel the coolness of her arms around him once more.

Like a blasphemer, Thomas closed his eyes and prayed fervently for her resurrection, here and now, as he and the men stood shoulder to shoulder in the heat and sunlight of a mid-June morning. The sparrows and wrens flitted overhead, their songs a mockery of the silence imposed by this solemn occasion, an uneasy quiet which all living things ought to heed as a warning, for their end was near too, nearer than they knew.

🐦 🐦 🐦

After the burial, his mother's body boxed and lowered into the earth like a treasure that had never breathed and laughed and held him, Thomas pulled free of his father's grasp and ran. He ran at top speed through the open gates and past the palisades, through the fields of corn and squash and over the mounds of flowering tobacco leaf, sprinting into the woods where at last the bright mocking sun was denied entrance.

The earth stank of decay; overhead, a flock of blackbirds squawked their disapproval and took flight. In the shadows of the ageless pines taller than a ship's mast, he fell to his knees and wept like a girl, wept unashamedly, for no one could see or hear him. He cried until all the water in his eyes was gone, until his throat had no voice.

He jumped at the heavy touch of a claw on his shoulder. Thomas looked up through his tears and saw the Indian boy, the Strawberry Thief, grinning at him. Thomas threw off his hand and cursed the savage to hell. Standing, he swung a wild roundhouse right. The young Indian ducked the punch and laughed, thinking Thomas's rage nothing more than good sport. He stuck out his chin, as if to say, "Try to hit me again!"

"Taunt me!" Thomas screamed, lunging at the boy, who fell back and rolled over with Thomas on top of him. They tumbled through the brambles and roots of the forest floor. Whenever Thomas got a grip on him, the savage broke it. He was too quick and too strong, and soon Thomas was panting like a pony that had been ridden too hard, and he gave in. The Indian shook him, wanting more. Thomas shielded his eyes with his forearms and rolled over, his face in the dirt. He howled in pain: he had no mother. How could this young savage understand the pain Thomas felt, the hollow cavity where his heart should be?

The grunting Indian climbed upon Thomas, who got to his hands and knees, and rode him as if the English boy were a stubborn pony, all the while crying out and whooping like a wild beast. With all his might, Thomas pushed up and rolled over, unseating the Indian, who fell to the earth with a gasp. Thomas fell upon him, his hands at the boy's throat, squeezing. The Indian's eyes bulged, his tongue protruded; Thomas felt him clawing at the fabric of his shirt.

Thomas might have choked the Indian to death had he been prepared for the boy's next move. Grabbing Thomas by the shoulders, the savage got a knee on Thomas's chest and flipped him overhead. Thomas landed on his back with a thud, all the air knocked out of him. For a second or two, he could not breathe. Then he gasped for a breath and choked, coughing until he feared that he himself might die.

When he opened his eyes, the sky was a bright blue dome, the tops of the trees stood against it like green lace, and he was no longer angry. A blue peregrine falcon circled overhead, perhaps two hundred feet above the treetops, looking for a meal of pigeon. You should have come to church on Sunday last, Thomas thought, addressing the hunting bird: he recalled the thousands of pigeons that had passed by just before services had begun. The sharp thwang of metal meeting wood drew Thomas's attention back to the meadow he lay in.

The young savage's blade glinted as it stuck in the trunk of a small pine tree. He grinned. The Indian had added another bangle to his ear and seemed satisfied with himself. How did he find me again, Thomas wondered. He had to smile: all the Powhatans from miles around must have heard him screaming and thrashing about like a wounded bear. Thomas wished they could speak and understand one another.

"Are you going to attack me every time I come to the woods?" Thomas asked, expecting no reply. He sat up and hugged his knees to his chest. He felt better now, his pain gone with the fight. His arms ached but he paid them little attention. The coolness of the forest floor soothed the fever that had driven him here from the village.

"You flipped me like a pan-cake!" Thomas said, snapping his finger; an image of Matthew Garret lying flat on his back formed in Thomas's mind, clear and sharp. "Thank you!" he said to the puzzled savage. He tried to grasp the Indian's hand to shake it but the boy backed away, perhaps thinking the move some kind of wrestling trick.

Thomas stood and found a sharp stick with which to write. In the bare earth at his feet he carved the curved bow, or rainbow, which was the symbol of their friendship, at least as he understood it. The Indian boy was clearly delighted, but took the stick without a word and redrew the curved line, giving it a greater, clearer arc. He grinned and stood back so that Thomas might admire the improved earthen sketch.

"What does it mean?" Thomas asked. "Do you want a weapon? I can't give you one, not even a knife. It's against the law to arm a savage. I could be held in the stockade or whipped."

The Algonkian boy looked at the figure in the earth and then at Thomas. With a sudden turn, he ran and pulled his knife from the tree. He stuck it in the narrow leather belt tied around his waist. The savage held up one cupped hand, just for a second, then turned and ran down a narrow path in the woods. Intrigued, Thomas followed.

The savage leapt and ran through the woods like a buck, never stumbling; Thomas fell once, and the Indian stopped to laugh uproariously. They ran until Thomas had lost all sense of direction. Only the sun overhead gave him any idea where he was. They came to a clearing where a small hut had been erected of bent birch, covered with bark and hides. This was the boy's hidden home! Thomas suspected that he was being shown something no one else knew of. The boy opened the hide flap that served as the door and they entered the smoky dome.

The charred remains of a fire were visible in the center of the dirt floor, which the boy had packed down. Overhead a hole let sunlight in and smoke out. In a leather pouch suspended from a peg inside the door rested what Thomas took to be the boy's treasures, things which he carefully took out and handed to Thomas one by one. A Spanish gold piece. Where had that come from? The Spanish were supposed to steer clear of Virginia, which belonged solely to King James and Mother England. He took it back, then handed the English boy a sparrow's egg, pale blue and uncracked. Thomas pretended to drop it; the Indian boy fell to his knees to catch it. He was fast! With a frown of disapproval, the savage gingerly lifted the egg out of Thomas's palm and set it back in the bag. Next he withdrew a single bead, bright orange, which held no fascination for Thomas, yet the Indian boy stared at it as though it had fallen from Heaven. He returned it to the pouch reverently. He then produced what Matthew took to be a nugget of pure gold.

Ducking under the flap, Thomas took the nugget outside and held it up in the sunlight. The glint and gleam were unmistakable. "This is gold! Where did you find it? Show me."

The savage took a step forward, reaching for the nugget. He said something like, "No," but dragged out the "o" and spoke through his nose, so that the word almost sounded like a lament.

Thomas ignored him. "You must show me where you

found this!"

The boy reached for it; Thomas withdrew his hand. In one quick motion, the savage grabbed Thomas by the shoulders, planted his foot next to his and threw the English boy to the ground, using his hip for leverage. Thomas held onto the nugget. The Indian twisted Thomas's wrist until he hollered and released the gold nugget.

Thomas got to his feet and hurriedly sketched the bow in the earth with a stick. He then erased it with his boots. "You are no friend of mine!"

Turning his back on the Indian, he ran off through the woods, keeping the afternoon sun on his back, so that he headed southeast toward Jamestown. The overgrown trail cut him; prickly vines tore at his shirt and slowed his pace. Nothing looked familiar, not the rocks or even a rock-strewn brook he danced across to keep his boots dry. The pines stood close together here; there seemed no way out of the woods. He paused but heard only the impatient cry of a bluejay raiding a rival's nest. Panic blurred his thoughts; Thomas forgot what his father told him to do if ever he got lost in the forest. He closed his eyes and pictured his father in the tangled hold of the ship, lecturing on farming techniques, woodlore, and survival in the wilderness. He could almost feel the sway of the hundred-foot long ship, the darkness and the stench etched in his mind like the devil's own nightmare. What had Father said? Think, Thomas! You are lost ...

Get to the river! That's it; there's always someone traveling the river. Traders, planters, the Governor's men—everyone rides the river. Thomas cut straight south, sure to come upon the James in a matter of minutes. He pushed aside the brambles and wild berry bushes, ignoring their jabs and pricks. He swore never to have another minute's commerce with the savage. As if Thomas were a dog to be whistled for and dismissed at the whim of a heathen! What would his father think when he told him of the gold nugget?

Thomas walked for what seemed an hour. Thirst took hold of him like a demon: where were all those streams and brooks he was forever falling into when his mother ordered him to stay dry? His mother. Dead. It did not seem possible. He must not mourn her now. He must keep a clear head and watch for snakes.

At last he came to a break in the wall of trees. Ahead he saw a meadow, and sunlight streaming down upon the grass and bare earth. He ran too fast to be careful. There, just beyond the tame meadow, twisting like a green ribbon and alive with light and dancing fish, lay the river, broad and gleaming in the sun. Thomas paused to give thanks. He calculated the hour to be late afternoon, but where was he? How close to—or how far from—Jamestown? He ran to the river for a long cool drink. A cry from nearby startled him. He fell to the ground and raised his head to see savages, six of them, fishing the waters with spears. They stood no more than fifty feet from him, where the current slowed and a man could wade out ten or fifteen feet before the waters swallowed him.

The Indians had the distinctive half-shaved heads of adult men, letting the coal-black hair on the other side fall in one long tail to their shoulders. They were all burnished a handsome coppery tone by the sun and moved through the shallows with grace and speed, barely disturbing the current. The Indians were muscular and moved with the ease of a bobcat. Thomas was afraid to move until they filled their baskets and left. Where was he that savages should be fishing nearby? He must have turned himself around and wandered northwest, toward Powhatan's old village. Too frightened to move, he lay still and watched, the blood pounding in his ears like a drum.

The shadows grew long, and the fish stopped jumping; Thomas lay his head in his arms to rest, just for a moment. His head was heavy, and his eyes shut of their own will. The river sang a lullaby.

🗡 🗡 🗡

He awoke in darkness. His eyes refused to stay open at first, and it seemed that an army of angels flew high overhead, their lights guarding and guiding him. He sat up quickly and rubbed at his eyes; the twinkling lights remained. Fireflies! Thousands of them!

The chirruping of crickets rose to a crescendo and died. A sudden splash drew his attention to the river. In the moonlight, the current sparkled like a silver chain twisting on a bolt of funeral cloth. A big fish—a sturgeon five feet long and weighing almost as much as Thomas himself—leaped into the silvery light and splashed before disappearing under the glassy surface of the water.

He must have fallen asleep, but for how long? The darkness had lifted its veil; a weak grey light hung over the river and the land like a fog. An owl hooted. A bullfrog bellowed for a mate: "Bwoah, bwhoah, bwoah!" The snap of a twig alerted Thomas to the presence of a night hunter, a forest beast. Or was it an Indian? He tensed and lay still, listening, the sweat beading on his forehead. His head filled with the sharp sour odors of the shallow water, and a whiff of wild onions. He smelled the fear that was a part of him.

The fireflies had vanished. Crickets whirred, then hushed, and a breeze from the river caressed his face. He was terribly thirsty, but he was afraid to move, even to breathe. Another snap, the breaking of a dry twig just ten feet away, alerted Thomas to the presence of someone or something drawing nearer. His heart pounded, threatening to jump out of his throat. Listening intently, he turned his head, instinctively covering his face, expecting any moment to feel the cool blade of a savage at his neck. Thomas said a quick prayer and shut his eyes; all the fight had gone out of him.

"Son!"

His father's arms were solid as field stone but welcoming, enfolding Thomas in a bear hug that left him gasping for air. The rough tickle of his beard against Thomas's smooth face stung, but he did not pull away, and together they sat by the river, rocking slowly, arms around each other, safe and sound. His father smelled of tobacco and sweat and the deep musk of the woods, where sunlight rarely reached the forest floor.

"Son, you must never do that again." His father's voice was stern but quivered, shaking with emotion. "You could have been killed, Thomas. Swear to me before God you'll never run off again."

Thomas took the oath and stood, his legs aching. "I miss Mother ..."

Charles Spencer embraced his son, holding him as he hadn't since they first set foot on the muddy soil of Virginia. The story poured out of Thomas: the Indian boy, the gold nugget, their quarrel, and his escape. His father said nothing but handed his son a half-loaf of bread and a small wheel of cheese from a leather bag worn round his neck.

"We'd best go, boy. I've left the others on an Indian trail by the river."

They heard for the first time the yap and howl of a hound, and Thomas realized how they had found him so fast. The dog had tracked him. After greeting the other searchers, who slapped him on the back and called him a hero, Thomas took one last look at the river, a pale glow hovering over it like a shimmering yellow netting, and turned to catch up to his father. On the way back to Jamestown by canoe and on foot, they were joined by other men who had searched the woods and meadows for the boy, and the story of Thomas's adventure and his "escape" from the Powhatans reached the settlement at dawn, as they did.

Outside the palisades of the settlement, Mrs. Garret waved her apron at Thomas, who grinned until he saw Matthew behind her, giving him the evil eye. At the Powell cottage, Priscilla stepped into the dusty street and waved the albino piglet at Thomas. Her long blonde hair swirled beneath her cap and gleamed like gold in the bright morning sun. She kissed the pink snout of the beast until it squealed and wriggled free, whereupon she gave chase and caught it, laughing like a maiden possessed. Fortunately, the widow Powell did not emerge from the deep morning shadows of their mean little cottage. As several townsmen shook his hand and slapped him on the back, Thomas prayed that the talk of witchcraft might die and never be heard again. What would happen to Priscilla if her mother were declared a witch and shunned or jailed? He imagined taking her in to sew and cook and wash for him and his father, but he knew Charles Spencer would have no part of it, no matter how much he yearned to defy gossip and slander. It wasn't proper for a young maid to live in a house with two men, especially a recent widower and his almost-adult son. Thomas was old enough to know that the tongues of men and women alike would wag. His father would not be the butt of crude jokes, however unjust and ill-founded. Above all earthly wealth and property, his father possessed a pride and a natural dignity that gave strength to those who did the right thing, and emboldened those men who bypassed or overcame temptation, never falling prey to its dark and unyielding tentacles.

At their cottage, too quiet without his mother stirring inside, Thomas's father made a fire and cooked him eggs, cutting a slice of bread thick enough to feed all members of the Jamestown militia. He set the food on the boards that was their dining table and looked about for a spoon.

"You are unhurt, boy?" his father inquired once more. He found a wooden spoon and wiping it on his sleeve, handed it to his son.

Thomas nodded, so weary he could barely keep his eyes open. He scratched the bug bites on his arms, wondering at the number of them. He had fed an army of long-tailed gnats!

The boiled eggs broke under his spoon and yielded their golden yolks. He ate greedily and mopped up the yolk with his bread. His father handed him a mug of milk fresh from the cow; the cream on top was so thick the wooden spoon could float on it.

※   ※   ※

Thomas slept most of the day, an unheard of luxury and waste of time, a sinful display of sloth. Yet when his father returned from weeding the fields and watering the flowering tobacco plants, he did not scold his son, but rather asked if stew would do for supper. Thomas had never known his father to be so kind and caring.

"Court Day is tomorrow, Thomas," his father said, washing his face and hands at the door. "You are coming?"

Thomas nodded. The shame of hiding was too heavy a burden for a thirteen-year-old boy.

"The Garret boy says you'll be wrestling him, for tobacco."

Thomas looked away. The fire was about to go out, so he stood and added crisscrossed logs to the embers and blew. The smoke rose and made his eyes tear. Smoke leaked from the chimney in wisps that floated toward the peaked ceiling and hung there like clouds. What could he say? He wished his father had not found him until after the Court Day contests were over and the drunken men had gone home to their cottages to sleep.

"We made no wager," Thomas said. That much was true. Matthew had mentioned nothing about tobacco or any other prize going to the winner of their wrestling match.

Charles Spencer sipped his water and tossed what remained in the cup onto the dirt floor. "The boy's a blowhard. Still," he added, wiping the sweat from his eye, "you can't back down. Face him and do your best not to get yourself killed. Can you do that?"

Thomas looked up at his father, who flashed a quick grin. Thomas swallowed hard before speaking; his mouth was dry again. "How?"

Charles laughed. "Duck and roll, son. That's what I did at your age when a brute chose me to whip. Duck and roll. And grin like it doesn't hurt." He gave his son a shake of the shoulders, snatched a burning ember from the fire, and went out the door for a smoke.

Thomas watched the blue smoke of the quick-cured tobacco curl and rise from his father's pipe, his father's familiar shape framed by the doorway and the evening sun. The heat weighed on him; his eyes were heavy but laden with images. The Indian boy, of his age or a little older: what did he want of Thomas? Why did he alone have a secret lodge deep in the woods, halfway between the Indian village and Jamestown? What did the arch drawn in the dirt mean, and why did he show it to Thomas? Everything about the young savage was a puzzle to Thomas, who wanted answers.

His father called out a greeting to Nicholas Houlgrave,

a passing gentleman dressed in knee-high white stockings, shiny leather shoes, a tight crimson jacket, and a velvet hat. Peeking at him as he strolled by, Thomas scratched the insect bites and cursed the heat. How could Gentleman Houlgrave appear so cool and untouched by the season and the gnats? He leaned against the wall, then withdrew his hand; green mold grew on the walls of their cottage in the humid summer. The slime was cool and slick to the touch but some folks said it made them cough. Thomas once heard the laborer John Capper, the widow Powell's chief accuser, tell his father that she used the mold to make a poison, a notion Charles scoffed at, but Thomas wasn't so certain. He sniffed the mold; it had a deep earthy odor, like mushrooms. Mushrooms could kill you sure as any poison; everyone knew that. Thomas quickly stepped outside to wash his hands.

The village was bathed in the soft golden light of the setting sun; a halo shimmered in the tops of the tallest oaks. Starlings settling on the peaked roof of the church sent up a chatter. Soon bats would zoom by, taking their evening meals on the wing. If they caught in your hair, it had to be cut to the skull or you would die, Thomas had heard. John Capper was bald and claimed all his hair fell out the night the widow Powell lost her husband to a festering wound.

Ospreys nesting on the river flew by, their elegant white wings and tapered bodies a reminder of the angels who watch over everyone who is not lost or fallen. At his feet the hard-packed earth lay solid and pale golden, as if formed of the firmament of Heaven. In a moment of such lush beauty, Thomas stood with his feet firmly on the hard dirt of Virginia but with his head and heart soaring high above, dancing through the clouds with the hawks and eagles. He understood at such rare times what the savages must have felt since birth—this earth is paradise, however fallen is mankind. He shut his eyes and took a deep breath. He smelled the sweet bloom of apple blossoms, the hint of honeysuckle, and the satisfying odor of bread baking. Always, the sour-sweet breath of the river hung over everything. You could not escape the river; it was destiny and motion and the road to the future.

A swarm of biting flies buzzed and attacked, and he ran from them, racing round the cottages until they gave up and found other and less mobile prey, like the widower Hodges, who smoked and talked tobacco-raising as though it were an upstart religion worthy of debate. To the rhythm of the old man's curses, Thomas strode back home, and with his father's assent, buttered and ate another slice of bread. He fell asleep to his father's deep voice praying the Lord's Prayer, never hearing the "amen."

🐟   🐟   🐟

The morning broke early and bright. Bluejays squawked in the trees. A bold crow strode by their opened door and peered in as if he had forgotten the address and was expected for breakfast. Thomas opened the shutter and looked out. His prayer for a sudden gale had gone unheeded. He had to face Matthew Garret in a matter of hours. With one hand, he felt and squeezed his own neck, wondering how much force it would take to screw it off like a cork from a bottle.

"Make a fire, son." His father's voice was stern and weary.

The holiday was over; Thomas was no longer a hero. He stepped onto the dirt floor and scurried to the fireplace. "There's no wood," he said.

"Get some." His father's voice was as flat as Thomas's hopes.

Thomas went out the door and gathered an armful of firewood from the porch. He looked down the quiet street where a few chickens scurried and saw the widow Powell waving her broom toward the sky, as if threatening a diving hawk. Thomas stepped off the porch for a better look and saw nothing above her — no bird, nothing but sky. What was she doing? He wished he could withdraw but felt obliged to stand there, the wood growing heavy in his arms, and watch.

The widow danced a jig and blew a kiss skyward.

From the garden in her fenced yard she pulled up an onion, which she swallowed whole. When she blew out a breath, flame seemed to dance on the tip of her tongue for a second; Thomas blinked, and the flame was gone. An oriole flew to the widow and landed on her finger, pecking at it once. She bent near the yellow bird and whispered or blew into its ear before it flew off. Faintly the sweet voice of her daughter drew the widow inside to their cottage, and Thomas was released from the unpleasant civic duty of watching a neighbor engaged in what might be sinful activity. He ran into the cottage, tripping on the raised dirt at the door.

"What is it, son?" his father jested, "Savages come to claim what's theirs?"

Thomas dropped the firewood with a clatter and trembled making the fire. Charles tried to inquire further into his son's well-being, but Thomas insisted that he was fine and had seen nothing. Soon the fire was hot, and water for tea boiled in the kettle. They ate in silence, an uneasy quiet Thomas feared might be part of the spell Priscilla's mother had cast. What else had she done, and how could he judge what ought to be kept secret and what must be told? His world was a jumble. Without his mother to prod and coddle him, Thomas was frightened, certain he was unable to be a man but no longer a boy with a mother to care for him.

He dressed and walked toward the dusty village green beside his father in solemn dignity, praying that he might never be asked to speak of what he had seen and wishing that Matthew had suffered a fever in the night and was indisposed, trapped in his cot with only enough strength to reach for the chamber pot and heave ho. Then he remembered the hip throw the Indian boy had used to toss him to the ground. Could such a simple tactic work against his foe? Did David slay Goliath? He brightened and smiled.

On Court Day, the men of Jamestown poured into the dusty street with gambling, drinking, and wrestling on their minds. The few women who remained scurried for cover in the shade of stately oak trees; most dragged their husbands home before they lost what profits the coming fall might bring. Just a few years of tobacco growing had already taught most farmers of the weed that caution was paramount, and anything could happen between planting in March and the fall harvest. Drought, storms, tobacco bugs that stripped a plant of leaves in minutes, and disease that withered the plants from within. These things Thomas learned quickly from his father, who never spoke of the credit they might have and what they might buy with it until after the harvest, sale, and loading of tobacco onto ships bound for England. After the ships had set sail and the winds blew cool from the western mountains—that was the time for celebration. Yet men were weak and wagered profits they did not hold and lost them, owing their futures. Few men were forgiving of debts, and more than a handful served time behind bars for bad debts, drunkenness, and thievery, often under the influence of drink. Thomas saw these evils every day and thought no more of them than any boy would, yet they cautioned him to obey the law and heed the commands of his father. So today he would face the Garret boy, do his best to stage a good show, and pray to God to escape with his wits and his limbs intact.

The clatter of a ball striking ninepins drew the militia men and others to the green, where a keg had been rolled under the shade of an elm tree. Arguments arose and threats abounded, most of them good-natured bluffs, for these men were long on talk and short on action, as Thomas's father summed them up. They came to work hard for a few years, make enough money to hire others to labor for them, and, God willing, retire to an upriver farm where a man with money might drink and eat far too much until the Judgement Day. Few men had achieved such selfish dreams, and none had stepped up from the class that defined him when he first set foot on Virginia's muddy soil, but every man shared the dream of wealth, and they all grew tobacco to feed that selfish dream.

"Our dreams go up in smoke," his father teased him again and again, pointing to a man stoking his pipe. Thomas never laughed. He worried that the crop would fail or the curing barn would catch fire or the ships from England would never arrive, and they would starve and suffer like so many before them.

Two men brought forth their horses, which were rare in Jamestown and highly prized. A gentleman in fine hosiery and a plumed hat proposed a horse race around the palisades, three times, the winner to take two hogshead barrels of tobacco. Other wagers ensued, the horses were mounted, and the race started with a waving handkerchief, which spooked the mare. She never recovered and was thrashed by her owner, who lost more than tobacco in his wagering. When he rode off on her, she shied and stepped into the ditch outside the walls, coming up lame. The owner's curses rang through the air like the notes of a trumpet better left unplayed. Thomas's father covered his son's ears with the palms of his hands until Thomas threw them off.

His father laughed. "Pray for his repentance, son. But not now." Enjoying the spectacle, Charles turned his attention back to the center of the circle of men and beasts.

Two upriver men unknown to Thomas stepped forward to wrestle, first sipping the rum that sustained them. Stripped to the waist, they were lean, hard men with tendons of steel and cords of muscle in their limbs. Their skin was pale in the sunlight, and sweat ran freely down their faces and chests. One man, a grower and trapper named Clinton, brought his brothers, who bragged that he could pin a bull and flip a bear. Thomas had his doubts but had nothing to wager — he could not even bet on himself. A merchant stepped forth to see that the match went on fair and square, and a ring was drawn in the dirt. The first man tossed out of the ring or unable to continue lost. Across the ring, Thomas spied Matthew Garret, whose big dark eyes shone with glee at the mayhem about to take place. The boy had a bloodlust that rivaled that of the savages, Thomas thought. Why didn't he wrestle one of them? At least Priscilla Powell was nowhere in sight to witness his humiliation.

The wrestlers flung themselves upon each other and grunted like pigs, snorting in the heat and rising dust. The men watching cheered and hooted, whistling for their favorite. The match ended in the wink of eye; the smaller man was lifted by his belt and tossed out of the ring, a tactic Thomas feared Matthew might try on him. His father rested a hand on his shoulder and patted him once.

The wait while other men wrestled was excruciating, like a day in Purgatory. At last the merchant stepped forward and asked who among the boys would wrestle for sport. Matthew pushed his way through a wall of men and gave his name, challenging Thomas to do the same. When the men got a look at Thomas, they hooted and jeered; many walked away to drink the rum, uninterested in such an obvious mismatch. Charles called out good luck to his son, but shook his head at those who would have wagered on the outcome. Thomas noticed and lowered his head; at least his father could pretend to have faith in him. Wager something, Father, he longed to shout, but he held his tongue and fought the shake in his knees.

The sun burned down on Thomas's bare head. Matthew stepped up and said that they would wrestle for a hogshead of tobacco. Thomas spoke up, denying any such agreement. Charles stepped forward and suggested they wrestle for something else.

"What?" the portly merchant asked, wiping his brow with a white cloth.

"Pride."

The men broke into laughter and rum-soaked cheers. Matthew tore off his rough linen shirt and revealed muscles like rocks. He danced a little jig and cracked his knuckles as the observers cheered and hooted.

"Duck and roll, son," Charles whispered to his son. "And say a prayer. Now."

From the side of his eye, Thomas saw a flash of white and turned to see Priscilla Powell snuggling the albino piglet in her arms. The creature squealed. Thomas wondered if he might be making the same sound in a moment or two. Priscilla brushed away a long strand of blonde hair; Thomas noticed that Matthew and most of the men were transfixed by her as well. She was a beautiful, winsome creature as ethereal in appearance as an angel. The silence was uneasy, the men's eyes greedy and shiny with drink, yet Priscilla seemed not to mind the attention and stroked and kissed her piglet, who wriggled and squirmed and squealed until Thomas thought he might go mad. Didn't she have the common sense to go home? He wanted to call to her, "How many other maids do you see here? None! Go!" Yet he kept his tongue and bit his lip and offered a plaintive prayer that his life be spared and no bones broken, amen.

"We cheer for you, Thomas," Priscilla said, proclaiming her words above the din. "Thomas the Pig and me." She kissed the pig on the snout, to the groans of the watchers. When she smiled at Thomas, Matthew snorted and edged closer to his prey, Thomas.

"Come in the circle unless you're too scared to move." Matthew's words were harsh, spoken with hate.

Thomas wished he might stop shaking. His knees trembled as if he suffered a sudden attack of palsy. Surely the men watching would notice and laugh at him. He could endure anything but ridicule, even pain. He expected pain.

The ring in the dirt was redrawn and they entered it. Wary of the boy's strength, Thomas hoped to slip under him and trip him; he was quicker than Matthew, and smarter. He also weighed half as much and might be crushed in the boy's bearlike grip.

The merchant gave the signal. "Go to, boys!"

Red-faced and grunting, Matthew charged; Thomas sidestepped him and tried to trip him, but Matthew regained his balance without falling and whirled, reaching for Thomas, who slipped past, edging toward the outer curve of the circle. If only he could run away! Matthew charged again, and this time Thomas used the Indian boy's trick. He caught the stronger boy by the shirt, turned, and let Matthew's momentum carry him to the ground. They both rolled over and Thomas wriggled free. The men cheered his cleverness. He heard his father call out: "Good move, son!" He sounded surprised, and pleased.

"He wrestles like a savage!" someone exclaimed.

Matthew taunted him, luring him closer. "You're a mother's boy, Thomas Spencer. You drink teat milk." His dark eyes burned with fury. Huffing, he charged Thomas and caught him in the belly, knocking the breath out of him. They fell and Matthew climbed on top, hissing curses in his foe's ear.

Without thought, Thomas worked his foot under Matthew's belly and grabbed him. He rocked forward just a little, then rolled back, holding onto the bully's shirt, and sent Matthew flying over him. The exhilaration terrified Thomas. He had never felt so strong. The crowd cheered. He heard his name raised in praise. Thomas was tempted to bow when the brute knocked him down from behind. He felt helpless as Matthew pulled back on his forehead and grabbed a foot, making a bow of him. Thomas could not resist; his back would surely break any second. He couldn't make a sound. His eyes filled with tears. He gasped for air. His neck creaked.

The release was divine, like being born all over and knowing it. Matthew fell off him as if struck by the Hand of God. Thomas turned to see his father reaching down for him.

"That's enough. Let's go home, son."

His father had never looked so tall and so strong. Even Matthew had the sense to keep quiet and let them go without a word of protest. The men cheered both boys and drank a toast. Thomas could barely get to his feet and found that without his father's steadying hand, he was dizzy and could barely walk a straight line.

His throat was raw and tight. Water would taste like the coldest cider, he thought. He put another foot forward and caught sight of Priscilla Powell, who blew him a kiss. He burned and blushed and wished his father did not notice but knew he did. Was she as mad as her mother? The heat in his head burned away all thoughts of his defeat. Should he tell his father what he saw Priscilla's mother do, dance fire on the tip of her tongue like a demon? Call to a bird and whisper instructions in its ear? Sorcery! Madness!

The walk through the dusty streets of Jamestown, past the mean cottages and gardens burned up by the sun, left Thomas weak and uneasy. If he could not speak freely with his father — and about some things, he could not — then how was he any better off than an orphan indentured to a stranger? In his heart, he was alone and a stranger in a strange land. He had no one to confide in but God, and a boy had no right to expect fairness of God, who lived by rules no man could conceive.

He stepped into the deep shadow of their cottage and faltered. His father approached him with a cup of water; Thomas sat at the table holding a crust of bread, too weary to put it to his lips. His father spoke gently, without raising his eyes, as if the words stung him inside. "I am sorry—"

Thomas grabbed his father and hugged him around the waist. Tears filled his eyes. "I'm glad you knocked him down, Father. I only wish it was me who did it for you."

Charles Spencer burst into a merry laugh. "That's spirit, son. You'll do fine in this world, if the Garret boy doesn't break you in two first. You've done fine, boy! Fine."

❧   ❧   ❧

In the morning, Thomas and his father heard shouts and ran into the street to see what might be the matter. They ran with a small crowd of men toward the stockade just inside the fence, near a pair of cannons on the raised earthen bulwark.

Peering out from the bars of the stockade was a leathery old savage caught stealing. No one knew how long he would be held or how he might best be punished, so the man languished in the cell, his cracked and weathered hands wrapped around the iron bars as if by sorcery he might twist them into pliable reeds. He looked so intently at Thomas as he passed that his father pushed him on ahead. Something about the savage—the glint of his eye— reminded Thomas of someone or something else, but he could not say what or who.

Just ahead of them, a semicircle of men dressed for field work stood shifting their feet and pushing for a better view. Thomas drew back when he saw the cause of the excitement: the Westons' runaway African slave had been caught rooting for food in the swamps.

"He killed and ate my pig!" John Capper shouted. Others supported his claim. They had seen the slave kill the pig with his knife.

The terror in the black man's eyes made Thomas's heartbeat race, as if he were connected to the man somehow. A crowd gathered, even a few women stood and watched. The Governor read the sentence and the punishment: thirty lashes. Thomas cared not a bit for Weston, a haughty smug fellow with little penchant for work but plenty of opinions. He had money—his wife's money—and spent it freely. Some day he would be governor, he bragged. At Court Day, he rolled out a barrel of rum for all and whispered promises of wealth and power into the ears of men unaccustomed to such promises.

"Abraham, have you anything to say?" the Governor asked.

The black man shook his head. Tears rolled down his face. He hung his head miserably. Wasn't that punishment enough? Thomas wanted to yell.

"He don't apologize," Weston said to the crowd. "He's lazy." He took the whip and snapped it against the ground as two men tied Abraham to the post. Thomas could not watch. The first crack of the whip and Abraham's cry sent a shiver through him. His father caught up to him outside the chapel.

"Son! The man ran away, he broke the contract."

"I would run too. Weston is a swine!"

The slap stung his cheek and burned. His father withdrew, a collapsed look on his face, as if he had lost something precious through his own foolishness. Thomas sat under an oak and pressed his hands over his ears to shut out the snap of the whip and the cries of agony. Now he knew why the Indian boy had built a hut in the woods just for himself. No one could spoil it. No one could enter unless he said so. No one would ever be hurt there.

🪶 🪶 🪶

When his father came home from the fields that evening, he said nothing to Thomas, who served him in silence. A whippoorwill hoo-hoo-hooed in a tree and seemed to

Thomas to be the unbroken spirit of Abraham, who had to be taken to a pharmacist and revived with spirits after the whipping. Somebody said he would surely die; another man boasted that he would cut off the ear of any servant who ran away from his employ. His eyes sore and crusty, Thomas slept uneasily and dreamt of Hell, where the rivers ran red with blood and fire and a scream like Abraham's went unheeded, drowned out by the greater sorrow of all who had once walked the green and fragrant earth of the world above.

In the morning, Thomas and his father stopped at the blacksmith's shop, for Thomas had a painful sty in his eye. His father stood behind him, shifting from one foot to the other, anxious and troubled. Holding the hoes and rakes, he was eager to get to work and no doubt imagined all the natural calamities of the land befalling his fifty acres of gold leaf tobacco every moment they delayed.

The smith had powerful arms and a friendly face and beckoned Thomas nearer to the fire, within a few feet of the horseshoe he was pounding and shaping. Thomas marveled at the clang of the hammer against the iron shoe. The man must be deaf as a stone. The heat and steam of the fire burned Thomas's cheek but he stood his ground, just a foot from the smith, who swung the hammer like Ajax vanquishing all the foes of ancient Greece. Thomas's eyes watered, and he wiped at them again and again: how much longer, he wondered. His cheeks burned; the skin on his forehead had surely burned away, leaving his unsightly skull open for all to see. The smith paused in his work and approached him, peering into Thomas's face intently. Nodding, he sent him away.

In the sunlight, Charles looked closely at his son's eye. "The sty has burst. You'll be fine now." He paid the smith, who grinned and took the money. The clang of his hammer seemed to follow them through the streets.

The unsightly chore complete and his eyesight returned, Thomas blinked away the pain and walked to the fields with his father, working with him side by side all day. The tobacco plants were over a foot tall now, and each had a green knob or button that had to be nipped off every day. The plants had been thinned so that they grew low and yielded only eight to ten broad wrinkled leaves. Each cherished plant now had but one stalk.

"They look strong," his father said, clearly pleased. "With kind weather and rain, they'll ripen and turn color in three months and we'll be rich as we're ever going to be."

It was a remarkable speech for his father to make. Thomas had never heard him speak so hopefully of the future. The words sunk into Thomas's heart like the milk and honey of the promised land, and he was soothed.

Thomas had healed from Matthew's thrashing, but the sun and the heat beat him down. He had to rest in the shade of the elms while his father hoed and weeded alone, the broad-brimmed hat so sweat-stained it appeared to be of two colors. His father complimented his work as they walked home at dusk, the sky jumping with unbroken chains of thousands of pigeons and quail.

Passing the Powell cottage, Thomas froze. The widow Powell was being led from her doorstep by a pair of town officials, the Governor's men. Thomas heard the word he dreaded above all others. "Witchcraft!" The wild, hurt look in her eyes as she was dragged past Thomas pierced his calm demeanor. The word staggered him; he reeled and was held up by his father, who looked grim.

He had to speak now. "Father!"

"Hush, son."

Priscilla ran into the street with her mother's white bonnet and apron. She raced after the men, who ignored her. Priscilla cried out for mercy but no one listened. She fell to her knees in the dirt and raised her hands to Heaven but people turned away, and her mother was soon out of sight. People passed her kneeling in the dust, clutching the white apron and bonnet, but no one offered to help, and Thomas was soon pulled away by his father, who was in no mood to debate propriety.

♠ ♠ ♠

That night, as his father snored in the bedstead beside his pallet, Thomas crept out of the house and up the moonlit street to the Powell cottage. As he suspected, Priscilla sat upright in the bed; through the open window, he saw her, her chest heaving, her eyes covered by her stark white hands. She seemed about to weep with every breath.

"Priscilla!" he whispered.

She ran to the window. "Thomas!" Her eyes shone in the moonlight; she took his hand in hers and held it. Her hair spilled over the top of her sleeping gown and fell down her shoulders and back like a golden waterfall. Thomas inhaled and grew dizzy. She smelled of lilacs. Her touch was cool.

"I'll do something," he said softly. "I promise you. I'll do something."

"Mother's mad," she confessed. Thomas wished she had not spoken. "She's no witch, no more than any old woman left alone too long with herself and a daughter and a thousand mindless chores. Do you understand, Thomas? We have no food and no money. The others won't give us their laundry."

He nodded. "You'll have our laundry, I swear it. Tomorrow. God will protect your mother." If she is innocent, he thought, but did not speak aloud. His heart beat like a captured bird's.

Priscilla said nothing but raised his hand to her lips and kissed it once. Her lips were cool, yet her tears on his skin set him aflame. He had to leave and pulled free of her cool grasp.

He walked back quietly as he could. He had taken but ten steps from her window when a shadow stepped forth and hit him with the force of a shovel. Blood flowed from his nose onto the ground. The world spun and his head buzzed with a score of bees.

"Speak to Priscilla again and I'll kill you. I mean it!" Matthew stood ten feet tall in the moonlight. His voice cracked with anger. Thomas feared for his life and shrank further into the dirt. Matthew shook his fist once in Thomas's face; it looked like a ham, fat and hard. When Matthew withdrew, his boots scuffed the earth like the devil's hooves, making a menacing sound even in the distance.

Thomas limped home and bathed his nose before bandaging it as best he could in the dark shadows of the cottage. His nose was puffy and swollen. It throbbed with every beat of his blood. What would he tell his father in the morning? He prayed for clarity of thought and mind, asking God to forgive him and his weakness. Was he doing right in caring for Priscilla, or were his motives tainted by desire? He wondered if all these misfortunes were not part of a plan to drive him into a cell of aloneness, as his father lived, as the widow Powell lived. Why must people suffer so at each other's hands?

＊　＊　＊

In the morning a blood-stained rag waved in his face. His father held it. His face was grim.

"Explain this."

Thomas took a gulp and told the truth, explaining that Priscilla had no food and was shunned by the village. "I promised her our laundry."

"Ah, son; the world's no place for kind people." His father sat at the table and looked out the open door, although his gaze was fixed on some faraway point. "Go on," he said softly. "Take the shirts. But don't speak to her."

Thomas gathered their dirty shirts and threw them into a basket. He carried them to the Powell cottage and left them at the door, knocking as he dashed away. He did not see Matthew but heard the door creak as he raced to catch up to his father.

Thomas thought about the Fall of Man all day as they yanked weeds and watered acres of tobacco plants. Did Adam and Eve leave Eden for this misbegotten world of woe? What manner of cruel God would do that to His own creatures, however fallen and disobedient?

He said nothing to his father. His nose began to bleed late in the afternoon, so he lay down beneath an oak and fell asleep, dreaming of a field of daisies and wildflowers in bloom, and there wasn't a soul in sight, nothing but the sun and the flowers and an invisible hand moving through the grass.

Chapter Four

THE RIVAL

The water was warm and the mud sucked at his feet; to move required more effort than Eagle Owl wanted to make, but fishing was something men did together, acting as one, like a wolf pack on the hunt. Flies encircled his head and buzzed in his ears; he ignored them and their stinging bites. Trapped bass, trout, rockfish, catfish, shad, perch, and sturgeon thrashed in the silk grass dip-nets that held them, their silver and blue and rainbow-colored scales glinting like jewels in the sunlight. He wanted to return to the village and question the healer about his dream. Why was it false prophecy? Can a boy who is son of the werowance have a vision that enlightens and inspires, yet lies? Eagle Owl felt conspired against, and ignored. His mother had urged him to mend his nets, and he took her meaning to be exactly that and nothing more; he stood waist-deep in the sluggish green river, dipping his net with his father and the other men in canoes, feeling the tug and pull of the fish in the net and the steady dull force of the river, a dumb beast that would live forever, like Powhatan and the other great chiefs who had flown over the mountains to rest with the gods near the sun.

"Eagle Owl!" His father shouted at him as if he were a child reaching for a burning ember. He straightened for a moment; his father's voice pricked him, stiffening his spine. His father pointed to his canoe, which was drifting in the current. He ran splashing through the shallow water and climbed in. He bent to the task of netting the trapped fish, which jumped and thrashed against the stick-and-reed weir entrapping them. A three-foot long sturgeon thumped against the side of the canoe; he struck it on the head with his spear once, twice, and pulled it in. He was lagging behind the other men who had cast their small nets against the current, snatching the fish that swam toward them like glittering breathing gems. Back in their village, great baskets would be filled with the smoked and dried fish, which would feed the people for weeks to come. The intruders, who were too busy growing tobacco to fish or hunt, would come to the people's long houses in the winter and beg for fish and corn, offering axes and beads. Trades would be made, but no man is pleased to give away food meant for his family. Eagle Owl feared trouble and foresaw enmity and bloodshed. Only his vision and his friendship with the pale intruder gave him any hope.

A cry of cranes drew his attention. He looked up to see a V-shaped party of the skinny white birds flying over like the spirits of great priests. Let them be a sign of good luck, an omen of peace and prosperity, he prayed. The birds made no sound as they disappeared beyond the trees.

A canoe of intruders came into sight, going upriver. The canoe was overloaded with hoes, shovels, and a wooden barrel that sat between two dirty and frightened men. Eagle Owl could see no muskets. The canoe rested low in the water; the barrel must be heavy, Eagle Owl thought. The pale bearded men struggled to paddle past Eagle Owl and the other Algonkians. The look in their eyes, a wariness mingled with fear, troubled Eagle Owl, who took no solace in terrifying another man, however foreign and foolish.

The Englishmen going upriver said nothing and looked back many times after they had made their way past the weirs and the canoes of the people. So little of what they did made sense. They defied the seasons and saved no food for the winter. In the spring when the leaves returned to the trees, they were lean like the Algonkians but they complained, as if their cries could speed the growth of the corn and squash they planted too soon or too late. Intruders cursed their fate but avoided the work that would improve it. They were men of little sense who did not belong in the land of the Algonkian people.

At his father's signal, the men paddled to shore and carried the nets and baskets up onto the muddy banks. Together, they lugged the heavy baskets teeming with fish down the winding path to the village, where the women waited to clean and smoke the fish and put it away. The trail was just wide enough for one man to walk quickly. Walking side by side with his father, he had to step over and through vines and prickly shrubs that tore at his flesh and hair.

At the village, Great Eagle went alone into his house. Murmurs ran around the village — a messenger from the Great Chief of the Powhatans, the Pamunkey leader Opechancanough, had come to tell them something. Men gathered around the werowance's yehawkin, with the women and children in an outer circle. Nobody spoke; the children danced and whined to go play but their mothers held their hands firmly and hushed them. Eagle Owl found his mother's eye: Oholasc looked worried. Little Dove and her younger daughters shied away from him. They had no doubt heard of his false dream and were warned to avoid him for a while, until he had regained his father's good graces. Quiet Lark emerged from their yehawkin to smile at him before her mother shooed her inside.

After what seemed hours, with the sun sinking behind the tall pines, the messenger emerged with Eagle Owl's father, who told them that one of their men had disobeyed the great chief's command and traded weapons to the intruders for rum. He was to be beaten and driven out, no one was to feed him or offer shelter. He gave the man's name: Dark Moon, a man who lived among the intruders more often than not and wore their boots. No one spoke against the order. Eagle Owl's father nodded to the messenger, saying that they understood. The man would no longer be given food or shelter in the village of Quiyoughcohannock. The man nodded and was fed by a fire in the heart of the village. Soon he would be on his way back to his village upriver.

Eagle Owl caught the eye of Little Dove, who looked sternly at him, betraying no emotion. Her eyes shone like black gold. He glimpsed the smooth brown back of Quiet

Lark slipping into her family's yehawkin with a basket of fish. Eagle Owl wandered to his house. His mother waited inside. She no longer wore the smile he was accustomed to seeing.

"Eat. Don't say a word to me." Her words were sharp.

"You're angry at me for the dream. It was true! I was the bridge—"

"Eat now. You have hurt your father. A man doesn't talk when he has been corrected by the werowance. He hushes."

Eagle Owl sulked, picking at the smoked fish, which crumbled in his fingers. Smoke from the fire stung his eyes; he deliberately let bits of the flesh fall into the fire. His mother pulled them out, casting a wicked glance at him. He nibbled at the corn and squash she placed before him in a bowl.

"Did you fish with your father?" she asked.

He nodded.

"Good. Kill a deer. Take it to your father and ask his forgiveness. Bring another to the priest."

Eagle Owl had to smile. "You would have me hunting until the snow falls." When Oholasc ignored him, he got up and went out to find his father, who was huddled with the old healer near the burial temple. A sudden gust of wind blew two reed baskets end over end. A storm was coming, fast. Eagle Owl looked up and saw the gathering purple clouds. Thunder rolled and boomed, and a crack of lightning broke. He grinned, welcoming the big storm. The world needed a cleansing. The gods knew that it was time.

Eagle Owl dashed toward the temple and tripped over something, falling to the ground with a thud. He looked up to see Grey Hawk grinning at him, laughing wickedly. Eagle Owl got to his feet and looked up at the taller boy, who flexed his muscles and took a wrestler's stance.

"You are clumsy like a cow," Grey Hawk teased. "And you lie. Quiet Lark will be mine."

Eagle Owl was about to jump him when his father called to him sharply. "You are wrong about everything, Tiny Sparrow," Eagle Owl said, addressing the tall husky boy blocking his path but looking to his father. He turned his attention back to Grey Hawk, who almost danced with anticipation of the fight. Grey Hawk had a strange way of turning his head this way and that, like an owl, as if he might see deeply into a man from a different angle. He stood sideways to Eagle Owl, and his piercing eyes bored into the chief's son. Four other boys had gathered to watch. Eagle Owl glared at them, saying nothing.

"Ask forgiveness for your lies," Grey Hawk told him. "or fight me now. Show me you are no fool."

Eagle Owl was tempted to wrestle him now and get it over with. He had little hope of beating Grey Hawk, but a good showing would calm the boy and cool the heated talk of marrying Quiet Lark. Eagle Owl's standing with the older boys would rise too, if he managed to stay on his feet and to hold onto his head.

His father called again, clearly angry. He was the werowance; he was to be obeyed, now. With Grey Hawk's taunts burning in his ears, Eagle Owl ran to catch his father, who was walking with a broad stride toward the river. "Bring the canoes in," he ordered.

"They are safe, father."

"Come with me."

Birds flew haphazard windblown courses along and across the river, squawking and seeking shelter. They were blown about like leaves. Raindrops fell hard as pebbles on the men. The rain hissed as it struck the dry earth. Soon they could not see across the river; a grey curtain of rain had fallen suddenly. High up, a hawk cried out. What did he mean, Eagle Owl wondered. Was he greeting the storm as well? The odors of wet earth and smothered cooking fires were strong.

"Talk to the healer," his father ordered. The rain did not bother him. He looked about with open eyes while Eagle Owl could barely see ten feet ahead of him. "He will take you back if you repent the false prophecy."

Eagle Owl swallowed, remembering what his mother had told him. If he disobeyed, he could be outcast like Dark Moon. He spoke softly: "I cannot."

"You must! Soon you will leave us. Your mother will weep." Great Eagle spoke loud enough to be heard over the pounding of the rain. His face showed nothing.

Eagle Owl understood. After the ceremony of entering manhood and months away from the village, he would return to live as a man and to marry and make a new family. He might never sleep in his mother's house again. "The huskanaw." The ceremony of separation, where boys were tested, and those who survived became men.

"Enough. If you are to be a man, you must heed me and the healer, and listen to the ancestors who speak through us. They speak clearly. When they do, you must take another path."

"Father, I know—"

"You know nothing. You have seen the leaves fall fifteen times."

"You wed at fifteen."

"You are not a werowance. I obeyed the healer and my father. I watched and learned. I said little. I tell you this: soon the time will come when you must heed me and you will not want to. Your heart may tell you to flee. But you cannot. You must do as I say."

With Eagle Owl trailing behind, wondering when they were going to seek shelter from the storm, his father touched each canoe, moving one farther upshore and into the shelter of the trees. Satisfied, his father spun and walked with long graceful strides back toward the yehawkins. Eagle Owl ran after him. The rain and wind drove them back to the village blindly. His father moved much more quickly and with surer steps; Eagle Owl struggled to keep him in sight. His father seemed to dance through the woods like a fox teasing the hunter, confident of escape.

Inside the smoky yehawkin, his father ate in silence as the children played, when not cowering in fear at the thunder. Their mother hushed them and told them stories, singing hunting songs Eagle Owl had not heard since the winter storms.

His father beckoned him with a look. "Tell me you will obey me. See the English boy no more. The match with Little Dove's daughter is uncertain. You are challenged by Grey Hawk, who is a more skillful hunter and fisher."

"He tripped me and accused me—"

"No more! Do you hear me? Tell me what I must hear from you. Tell me now."

Eagle Owl looked to his mother for help. She avoided his glance, clapping hands with the children, singing a silly song about the fox and the turkey, leading the little ones in a foolish dance around the fire. The thunder boomed and the children screamed again, but with delight. Rain drummed on the house and pounded the earth outside.

He shook his head. His father threw down the bowl of squash and fish. The food fell onto the dirt floor. His father's eyes glowed with anger. "Go."

Eagle Owl glanced at the rain pounding just outside the house. He could not see the nearest long house and looked back to his father. "Now?"

"Go."

With a plaintive look at his mother, he stood and gathered his bow and knife. "I am sorry, father."

His father pushed him out the door with a powerful shove. Eagle Owl stumbled in the mud and slipped down the path to the river. He had no choice now. He might lose his family, his place in the world, his chosen mate—yet he would tell the truth. The vision was his. If it were false, he would be false and may as well be dead.

He found his canoe and pushed off quickly. The rain danced on the waves blown by the wind. He could barely see. His canoe rose and fell in the waves. The paddle cut through the grey chilly water, lashing the air when the boat rose. Eagle Owl enjoyed the feeling: alone, on the water, lashed by the wind and rain. The rain kissed him; the skies wept for him; he belonged here. He paddled hard for the far shore. An otter raced by, glancing wide-eyed at Eagle Owl as though he were mad. Maybe he was.

What did his father mean about obeying when his heart would not want to? What was he planning with the other werowances? Were they going to rescue the old priest's brother from the stockade in the walled English village? He had heard such talk; Grey Hawk swore to lead such a rescue. That would be madness; the English had guns and cannons. Many would die. Namontack's brother would surely be freed soon, the misunderstanding cleared away like a storm blowing past the coast. Perhaps the English boy with the sky-colored eyes would help. He must talk to the boy again, teach him the words.

On the far shore, Eagle Owl hid his canoe in brush and ran up the narrow path to his small home. Inside, he tore at the smoked trout and held the gold piece so prized by the English boy in his hand. What did he want with it? It did nothing; it caught the sunlight and threw it back. On a rainy day, like now, it did nothing. The golden lump was useless as a bird with one wing.

He built a small fire and lay back in his house. Thunder shook the sky; someone was angry. He asked pardon, imploring the gods to give him a new and clarifying dream, and fell asleep in his wet breechcloth, having tossed his bow and knife on the dirt floor beside him.

✦   ✦   ✦

Grinning like a skull, Little Dove approaches him, her hands extended, cradling in her arms a gift wrapped in hides. He opens it: a bloody child falls onto the earth. He draws back and screams. Sparrows and hawks fly out of his mouth, and before his horrified eyes, the hawks tear the smaller birds to pieces. Blood gathers in a pond all around him and stains his feet red. The fallen bloody child opens his eyes; stars fill them. The stars swirl and join and form a silver ball, which rushes through the sky with a deafening *whoosh*!

✦   ✦   ✦

Eagle Owl awoke with a start. His heart beat wildly in his chest. The storm had passed. Cicadas whirred, and above him, squirrels clucked and chattered. He stretched and got up. He must gather nuts and berries. Let the fates lead him where they will. He lived alone now. He had no other home than the bark dome in the woods, on the intruders' side of the river. So be it.

He gave the dream little thought. When he was welcomed back into the village, he would ask the old priest what it meant. Until then, he had work to do. He shook the rain off. He must entertain himself now. He ran through the woods to a berry patch, keeping an eye out for intruders, and filled the pouch at his waist, all the while looking for the boy, hoping to see the lean young intruder. He might have been the other person in the world, the first man alone in the garden, awaiting the gods' creation of a mate. From him all men and women would flow like a river, and over him, like a bridge, they would walk into what was to come, or so he believed.

If he must be punished for his faith, very well: he would be punished. Eagle Owl found walnuts by the score and sat down to enjoy them. The sun broke through the haze and burned into him. A fog lifted above the forest floor and lazily hung in the air. The grass beneath him was wet and cool, pleasant to sit on.

Ahone, great god, I feel your smile upon me, he thought. He bowed in thanks and kept his eye on the trail toward the English settlement. A buck burst through the underbrush and jumped over him, nearly taking his head off with its hooves. The creature stopped just twenty feet from the boy and was met by a doe, which whipped her white tail and jumped to greet him. They ran off into the woods, leaping with joy. Eagle Owl laughed—such an obvious sign! He must go to his village back for Quiet Lark. She would join him here, now, forever!

Laughing with delight, he ran toward the river and his canoe.

Chapter Five

THE WITCH'S DAUGHTER

Tied to a rope trailing from the stern of a shallop, the widow Powell stood ankle-deep in the stinking mud. She wept bitterly but said nothing. Her wrists were bound before her; the hem of her white apron dragged in the reddish-brown mud. Two men in the small boat raised and lowered the oars and kept their eyes on the widow as if she might vanish. Longtailed gnats buzzed and bit the rowers, but the widow seemed undisturbed by the biting insects. The sun was lost in a haze that sapped a man's strength and soaked through his shirt in ten minutes of labor.

At the edge of the water, a crowd of men, seven women, and a few children had gathered to watch the widow's punishment. Two men openly called for her drowning. Thomas and his father stood near Priscilla, who was held by two women, one at each forearm. Priscilla howled pitiably, pleading for mercy.

"She's not a witch! She is ill! Mercy upon her soul!"

"Your silence does you no service," the Governor's man told the widow. His voice wavered; clearly, he did not like this duty and wished to be elsewhere. "Repent your sins and renounce your sorceries, and we shall release you. We wish you no ill. Your soul is in torment, that is clear for all to see. You have lost a husband, and for that loss, you have our pity. Yet sorcery is no substitute for proper behavior and Christian forbearance."

The widow turned away from the crowd, sniffling and whimpering, and looked across the scum-covered pond toward the pitch and tar swamp beyond it. Runaway slaves had escaped into the swamp but always returned, swollen by bites and shaken by encounters with snakes and ghosts. One African servant had not spoken a word since his capture in the tar pits. Only a witch or a madwoman would consider fleeing to the swamp.

The man in charge cleared his throat. A sweet-spoken fellow, he raised his voice so as to be heard by all. Clearly he did not want to punish the mad old woman trussed up like a Christmas turkey. "Widow Powell, you stand convicted of sorcery and of confluence with the devil. You have sickened children, shot hair balls into cattle, and turned men into horses. The muskets of those who stepped forward to accuse you no longer fire. Have you nothing to say?"

Several men in the crowd demanded her dunking. Thomas recognized the coarse mouth of John Capper, whose voice was as bold as his gleaming head. The Governor's man ordered them to be quiet. A woman spoke aloud a prayer for the widow's eternal soul. Priscilla wailed. The sun burned down relentlessly. A child in the crowd collapsed, overcome by the heat. His mother carried him in her arms to the shade; someone ran for water.

Thomas gripped his father's forearm. "Stop them." He looked at Priscilla, who was frothing at the mouth, tearing at the women who held her. Her moans and cries were horrible, like those of a beast roasting alive in a fire. She might be beaten at any moment or confined in the jail until her senses returned to her. He had to help her.

With the Governor's prior assent, the Reverend Wilson read aloud several ominous passages from the Old Testament. "'Thou shalt not suffer a witch to live,' says the Good Book in Exodus, twenty-two, eighteen. Leviticus twenty reads: 'A man also or woman that hath a familiar spirit, or that is a wizard, shall surely be put to death; they shall stone them with stones; their blood shall be upon them.'"

As the minister paused, flipping through scripture for another passage of guidance, Thomas saw John Capper reach for a rock. He called out, and the minister raised his hand.

"The Bible guides us and holds up our law as the

ocean floats the great ships from England," he said, eyeing the bald loudmouth directly, "but our law is kinder. Put down the stone, John Capper."

Capper grumbled but dropped the stone. He glared at Thomas and swore under his breath.

The Reverend took a deep breath and read further, flipping though the battered book with alacrity. "In Deuteronomy eighteen, verse ten, we read: 'There shall not be found among you any one that maketh his son or his daughter to pass through the fire, or that uses divination, or an observer of times, or an enchanter, or a witch.' The Good Book is clear! The Lord will not abide these abominations, nor shall we!" The Reverend nodded to the Governor's agent, who signaled the two men in the boat to row toward the middle of the scum-laden pond.

The widow looked straight ahead. Her lips trembled, as if she might speak. Her eyes rolled upward, toward heaven. She said nothing. The widow whimpered as her feet touched, then sank beneath the water, which crept up to her knees and waist. In a moment, the brackish green water splashed at her neck.

"Repent, witch!" a man cried. Others howled oaths at her. John Capper and two rum-drinking friends swore that she would float and could not sink, even with a stone tied to her chest. The minister called them fools and threatened them with a dunking of their own.

Thomas could not keep his peace. "She'll be drowned!" He shook his father. "Father, help her! Cut the rope!"

Charles Spencer watched with fascination, like the others, as the widow floated over the pond. "It's her doing, son."

Thomas bolted toward the muddy edge of the pond. His father was a step behind and held him back, pinning his arms at his side. He seethed with frustration and stomped the earth with his boots, looking for Priscilla, who was out of sight, dragged behind the semicircle of people gaping at the widow. Just beyond the periphery of the circle of men stood a pair of Powhatans, in high feathers and leather wrist guards, with an unfathomable look on their sunbeaten faces. Thomas could not tell if they approved or were amused or disgusted. Their faces seemed always the same: passive, composed, and serene, as if nothing on earth could destroy their resolve.

"This is the law, son!" his father hissed in his ear. "She won't defend herself. She gives us no choice."

"She is mad," Thomas hissed, tugging to escape his father's iron grip. "She needs bleeding, and medicine!"

The widow was into the water up to her mouth, her forehead, and at last, she disappeared under the foul green scum. A dragonfly hovered over the bubbles. Thomas noticed an oriole swoop low over the boat before flying away, resting on the branch of a willow hanging over the far side of the pond. No one but Thomas seemed to take note of the yellow bird, which watched the ordeal with interest and sang a little song of alarm, three sharp notes like a call to arms. Thomas shuddered, recalling the last time he had seen such a bird at the widow's cottage, just before her indictment. A flame had danced on the tip of her tongue then, yet now she would not speak even one word to save herself.

The dragonfly hovered over the bubbles in the pond.

"It's her soul!" a man cried, pointing out the insect to the others.

"Kill it!" John Capper yelled. "Shoot the dragonfly!"

One of Capper's friends raised his musket; Thomas's father stepped forward and shoved the barrel down, giving the man such a steely-eyed stare that he set the musket at his feet and pretended that he had no intention of ever firing it. Capper cast a look of hatred at Charles Spencer, who returned the favor.

Released by his father, Thomas looked to Priscilla, who lay collapsed and weeping in the dirt. He did not know whether to act or hold his ground, trusting in God to spare the widow. He hesitated, watching the bubbles rise to the surface of the pond. Every second seemed an hour.

The minister counted aloud to ten, then ordered her returned to land. The blue dragonfly whizzed away as the widow came up sputtering and coughing, her hair black and clinging to her eyes and face. Strands of scum dotted her hair and caught on her shoulders like decoration.

"Enough!" Priscilla cried. She ran toward her mother but was held back, by order of the minister. The Reverend studied the widow closely for signs of repentance, then withdrew.

Thomas echoed Priscilla's cry. "No more! She is punished!"

His father hushed him. Others called out for more. The minister asked to hear her repentance, and when she said nothing, did not hesitate to act.

"Again," he said.

The childlike whimpering of the widow seemed the only sound one could hear; everyone held his breath as the widow was dragged out into the water and soon fell from view. Priscilla had lost her voice and gasped for breath, her mouth thrown open in silent agony. Thomas could not look at her; his father gripped him harder than before. The widow took a great gulp of air before going under, and Thomas prayed that she might survive. The counting seconds passed too slowly. "Five ... Six ... Seven ..."

"Mother!" Priscilla's cry pierced Thomas's heart. He broke free of his father's grip and ran splashing into the water, startling the two men in the boat. He swam to them and tugged at the rope until one stood and whacked him in the ear with an oar. Thomas fell back with a splash and felt the warm flow of blood in his ear, and a hum in his head like a beehive. His father reached him and pulled him to shore as the signal was given to haul the widow out again.

The widow lay limp and sodden on the mud. Someone pronounced her dead as a stone. Priscilla howled and fell to the earth, beating her head against the dirt. Her face a mask of anguish and tears, she crawled to her mother on hands and knees.

Thomas ran to Priscilla, afraid to touch her. She cursed them all, casting one wicked oath after another, until Thomas feared that she too might be tied and dunked.

"Priscilla! No!" He took her hands in his but she wriggled free of him, twisting like a serpent, and hissed oaths no maiden should ever hear much less speak aloud and in public. Thomas recoiled, as if struck by her spite. His father took him by the arm and pulled him away. A murmur ran through the crowd.

"She's alive! The witch is alive!"

Thomas and the others who had turned their backs on the pond spun to see the widow released of the rope and pulling at the collar of her gown as if it were strangling her. She stood with great effort and fell forward into the dirt, spitting and coughing. A small pool of water gushed from her mouth and darkened the earth. Her daughter pushed aside those in her path. Priscilla covered her mother's head with kisses and lay across her as if shielding her from a rain of arrows.

The minister called for the crowd to disperse. Thomas wanted to remain, to see if Priscilla wanted a hand and to show her that he would defy convention to help her, but his father insisted that they get on with their work.

"The widow is alive. Let her daughter tend to her," his father said, looking away. He too seemed troubled by the ghastly scene.

Breaking free of his father, Thomas ran home and wiped at the blood in his ear. The buzzing in his head relented, and soon he could hear bird songs in the trees and the soft play of the wind in the willows and oaks. The dizziness released him, and he got to his feet without swaying or stumbling.

His father found him resting with his head in his hands at the workbench and dragged him to their tobacco fields, where they weeded and hoed and watered under the glare of the sun. They spoke not a word to each other; Thomas thought his father might as well have been a Chinaman or the Pope, for all they had in common. When would his father stand up for what was right, no matter the cost?

That evening, at dinner, his father warned him. "Do not be seen in the company of the witch and her daughter."

"She is not a witch, father!" Thomas almost shouted. "Didn't her dunking prove that?"

"The preacher, the Governor, and the burgesses are wrong and you alone are right, eh? What kind of false pride is that? Pride goeth before fall, son."

"Don't cite scripture at me, father; it doesn't become you."

Thomas reeled as his father raised the back of his hand but held it, trembling. His father blinked and slowly lowered his hand; his mouth was tight and small.

Thomas ran out the door, running so fast the tears could not fill his eyes. The sun was setting on a shameful day; Thomas raced the shame out the gates and into the woods until he came to a clear stream. He dove in and swam until he could not breathe. Coming up for air, he saw the last pale purple streak of light in the sky die to black, and in the shimmering night air, the tortured face of Priscilla Powell lit up the darkness like the lonely Maiden of the Moon.

🝆 🝆 🝆

When he returned after dark, his father was snoring. After changing into dry clothes, Thomas crept out of the cottage under the moonlight and filled his arms with firewood. He tiptoed down the street to the Powells' cottage and gently laid the wood at their doorstep. As he turned to leave, the door opened and there stood Priscilla in a white linen nightgown that swept the floor. Her hair fell far past her shoulders and swayed with each movement of her head. She appeared composed and spoke softly, with great tenderness. Her eyes sparkled.

"Thomas, how kind of you."

"I'll bring tobacco, soon. And meat."

"Come to the window. I have something for you." She turned and disappeared inside the cottage. He could see a rush light glow and through the cracked door, her mother lying on the bed, unmoving. Her suffering reminded Thomas of his mother, and the deep pang of her loss struck him again. A sharp arrow struck inside his chest, in the heart.

"Here."

Through the open window, she handed him a vial of crushed herbs. "For your father's temperament. And your own."

Thomas was disappointed; he had hoped for something

more personal, a cameo or a pin of hers. Or a hairbow with her scent upon it. "I'll never get him to take it."

"Slip it in his tea when he's not looking."

She laughed once, touched his cheek with her cool ivory hand, and closed the shutters. Her touch inflamed him. He ran home without looking back. Removing his boots at the door, he crept inside as quietly as possible. He pulled back the netting and was about to fall into the lumpy mattress when a hand gripped his arm fiercely. Thomas cried out.

"You disobeyed me!" his father said, his voice harsh and unforgiving. The first slap caught Thomas by surprise; he covered his face thereafter, and the others did not sting so much.

Thomas feel asleep with the salt of his tears in his mouth. His cheeks stung, and one eye was filling with blood, where his father had caught him flush with his hard knuckles. He prayed for justice and for his father to join his mother in Heaven so that he might marry Priscilla and carry her upriver, away from Jamestown and the pond and a hundred watching eyes. He almost wished Priscilla's herbs were poison.

🐦 🐦 🐦

The thought struck him like his father's first slap; he sat bolt upright in bed and knew just what he must do. He dressed and slipped out the door to his father's broken snoring.

The woods were bathed in the silver light of a waxing moon; he could see quite well enough, if only he could remember the twisting hidden path. A hundred Indian trails led every which way to and from Jamestown. How could he hope to find the right one? A silly thought occurred to him —perhaps his wrestling foe, the Indian berry thief, would find him. Were they friends now, or enemies? He had forgotten.

Thomas ran through the woods with abandon, allowing instinct to guide him. His father would be furious if he got

lost again: another day of work sacrificed, men to be gathered for a search and to be paid for their effort, the humiliation of a son who would not heed his father. Thomas
might well get another beating. No matter—he had a mission. He had to find the small Indian house and return
home before dawn.

Ahead on the trail, a whippoorwill flew along the darting path, as if guiding him. He followed. After stumbling for
what seemed hours, he came to the hut half-expecting it,
half-amazed. He laughed aloud. Thomas jumped for joy,
wondering where the gold was hidden. With it in his hand,
he could prove to his father that there was gold nearby,
and with the berry thief's help, they might find it and be
rich. Maybe the gold lay in the mountains to the west, land
Thomas longed to see and walk.

Outside the hut something moved in the shadows.
Thomas drew back, but too slowly. Something rock-hard
thumped against his head, and he fell to the ground after
glimpsing a tall savage looming over him in the pale grey
light.

🪶 🪶 🪶

The knob on his forehead throbbed. He rubbed it. One eye
was all but shut and swollen with blood. Could he get any
uglier? He heard voices, strange, hushed mumbles. What
were they saying? Where was Father? He tried to rise but
found his hands and feet bound. He struggled but the
leather bindings only seemed to tighten against his flesh.

He opened his one good eye and could see in the dim
light of dawn that he lay inside a long house, the domed
structure of the Powhatans. There was a fire in the center
of the dirt floor; skins and hides were piled high on raised
wooden platforms all around him. He seemed to be alone
inside the twenty-foot long, loaf-shaped Indian house.

His head ached. He could not rub it. Every thought
seemed to cause pain, but he had to think. Why was he
seized? He had nothing of value. "I am just a boy!" he
thought to scream. But who would understand him? Some

Indians understood some English but most did not, or pretended not to.

Someone drew back the reed flap covering the doorway and entered the house. A smile, here then gone. Lean, quick as a cat—the Berry Thief!

"Untie me!" Thomas whispered. He rolled over to hold up his bound wrists. The Indian boy did not move.

Behind him came a tall muscular Indian man with a great sheaf of feathers sprouting from his head, which was half-shaved. The Indian looked as if he could pick up a mountain and put it where he wanted; Thomas had never seen such muscles. He had captured Thomas: but *why*? He sent the boy out and spoke to Thomas firmly but kindly in a tongue he did not understand. With his hands, he gestured; Thomas understood that they had taken a canoe trip, perhaps a reference to his crossing the river last night, a journey he had no recollection of. The Indian held up his fingers: the palisades at Jamestown? He walked in with one hand and out with the other. A trade? They would trade Thomas, but for whom? He thought: the old Indian held for thievery. He was proposing an exchange.

Thomas tried to warn them. He mentioned the cannons and muskets and made the noise, "BOOM!"

The Indian laughed. "BOOM!" he shouted in return, startling Thomas. They both laughed. He made the motions of eating with his fingers and left. Soon a handsome woman in buckskins entered with beans and squash and fish in a bowl. She fed him with her fingers. He ate hungrily.

With the hide door open, Thomas watched the Indians pass to and fro. They seemed hardly savage; most carried game or food in baskets. The boys chased each other and laughed like English boys at play. Women and girls carried hoes to the vegetable fields he had seen and heard about.

🔸 🔸 🔸

That night, Thomas was nudged awake; a hand stinking of fish clamped over his mouth. He half-expected a knife at his throat and said a quick prayer, asking mercy upon his soul. He opened his eyes and saw the boy by the wavering firelight. The Berry Thief put a finger to his lips. Pulling out his knife, he cut loose the leather ties. In his hand was the gold nugget. Thomas could not speak. He thought to give the boy the cross around his neck on a leather string and did so.

"Thank you, my friend," Thomas whispered. "May God bless you."

The Powhatan knelt in the packed dirt with the captive English boy and once more patiently drew the rainbow symbol with his finger. Thomas anxiously peered at it. What if someone found them now? They would both be punished. Using one hand, the Indian moved his fingers up and over the rainbow sketched in the earth, like a crab scuttling back and forth over a bridge. He held that hand behind him and did the same with the other. Then, both hands crossed the bridge, passing each other slowly and touching. At that moment Thomas understood: he was to be the bridge of understanding between their peoples, he and Thomas. Both worlds could learn from each other.

"I see!" Thomas almost cried out. The Indian he knew as Eagle or Owl clamped a hand over his mouth. Thomas inhaled deeply and nodded, meaning he would make no more loud noises. The boys embraced.

"We are brothers," Thomas whispered, deeply touched by the Berry Thief's courage. "I won't forget."

The Indian boy nodded. He said something that Thomas took for "brother" in Powhatan. They both smiled.

After examining their gifts in the pale moonlight, he led Thomas silently out of the village, to the edge of the fields, where the trail led to the river. Thomas understood that he was to take the boy's canoe.

"But what about you? You will be punished."

The Powhatan seemed not to understand and hurried Thomas along, shoving him hard. Thomas raised a hand in goodbye and the boy vanished.

He rowed across the river in the darkness, wondering at his freedom and its price to his Indian friend. He must visit the old man in jail and try to free him. The gold! He held the nugget in his hand. Perhaps now his father would let him journey west to the mountains. If not, he would take Priscilla as his wife, and together they would find gold and the China Sea.

Thomas smiled at the thought. A cloud released the light of the moon, which glittered and broke upon the river. He heard the splashing of beavers nearby. They too had work to do. But what of Priscilla's mother? A shiver shook him, and cold water ran up his spine; he had no room in his dream for a old madwoman. How could he persuade Priscilla to leave her behind? How could they live together happily with a madwoman?

He heard another splash behind him and paddled hard for the far shore. The cowardly moon ducked behind another dark cloud and the darkness engulfed him. When he shifted his weight in the canoe, the gold nugget bit him in the thigh. He dug it out and popped it into his mouth, eager to show it to his father and to Priscilla. Maybe her mother would tell them to go and give them her blessing: gold had a power over people.

That was it! He pushed at the nugget with his tongue: it felt smooth and heavy and magical. If he showed Priscilla the nugget and told her his dreams, she would follow, and all would be well. He paddled for shore with renewed strength, his wake cutting a silver stream in the sleepy grey river.

Chapter Six

EXILED

He found Quiet Lark sleeping and woke her with a touch. She made no sound, though her eyes grew big, and followed him outside. Under the heavy yellow moon, he whispered his love to her, speaking feverishly. His talk was so wild that she withdrew, recoiling.

"You must come with me now!" Eagle Owl insisted. "We will live alone, like the first two people. Come!" He tried to drag her with him, toward the river. She shook her head, her eyes wild with fear, though she could not pull free of him. She whimpered once, and he slackened his grip. "In my dream—"

"Let her go!" Little Dove snapped. She stood just outside their yehawkin. In her hand the blade of a knife glinted.

Eagle Owl was startled. Quiet Lark broke free of him and ran to her mother, who enfolded the trembling girl in her arms. From inside their long house came her other children, one by one. Their sleepy eyes accused him of madness and treachery, and Eagle Owl had no words of explanation or apology to offer them. He was almost relieved when his father appeared. Of all the murmurs of disapproval from those who gathered to watch the werowance drag his son away by the hair, only Grey Hawk's smug laughter tortured him.

★ ★ ★

Eagle Owl did not duck the blows his father dealt, nor did he cry. His father's hand was hard as stone; it stung like a wooden club hitting the back of his head. His father denounced him as a fool and a dupe of the English boy.

"Did he promise you a musket? He lies!" His father's voice was harsh and sharp, a tone he reserved for shaming thieves and wantons.

Eagle Owl shook with fear. His father was very strong and might dislodge his brains or beat him deaf in one ear; such things happened. He cringed and said nothing. A warm breeze from the water blew across his skin, which stung from the blows. He smelled the mud from the bay and longed to run off and dig for clams with his toes, by himself. If his father ever let him go. He swung away but was not free, and another blow fell upon his head, then on his back. For how long could his father be so angry? He had defied his father, but to help a friend. Wasn't friendship sacred? How had he hurt his village? He dared to ask.

His father took a breath and let the words out slowly, seething. His chest heaved. "Fool! How are we to free the priest's brother from the English with no one to trade for him? Why should the intruders release him, because we ask? We have asked before! Because of your foolishness, the old warrior will die in chains."

Eagle Owl had not thought of that. Trading the English boy for the priest's brother made perfect sense. Why hadn't someone told him? He might have made the English boy understand, although he spoke no Algonkian and was pale as a maggot. Eagle Owl flushed and suddenly felt smaller, as if his ignorance had shrunk him.

The blows ceased. Eagle Owl slowly straightened and opened his eyes. His father had withdrawn a pace and stood looking east, toward the sunrise over the water. He spoke slowly, with no joy or pride in the words that came from his mouth. "You are banished. Take a canoe and go."

"When can I return?" Eagle Owl dared to ask. He looked once more at his father, hoping to see a sign of regret or sorrow in his father's dark eyes, but the warrior turned his back, folding his arms as if awaiting an expected birth—or death. He would not reply.

Eagle Owl rubbed a knot on his head and walked away. His feet were heavy and clumsy; he tripped more than once. The trembling ceased, and a bone-weariness inhabited him, like a spell cast by a powerful sorcerer. He could have fallen asleep on a bed of rock.

🦅　🦅　🦅

Inside his house deep in the woods, he slept and dreamed of life in his village across the broad river. The yehawkins he passed poured out smoke through the hole in the rounded roof. Already, he dreamed, women stirred; in one long house, a child cried, and someone stirred to hush her. Larks and robins sang; a squirrel ran down the trunk of a sycamore tree and froze when he spied movement out of one eye. He passed Little Dove's house and wondered what Quiet Lark's face looked like as she slept: was she smiling? Did she fear him? What would she say and do when she learned of his exile? Would she choose Grey Hawk in his stead?

He awoke and built a fire. The smell was of home and made him very hungry. He stood so near the water that he could hear the big river fish splashing in the morning sun. His bare feet touching the cool wet grass gave him some pleasure. Like a thunderstorm, his father's anger would pass. Were his father not the werowance, he might have been pardoned sooner—or punished more severely. Still, no boy was exiled forever. Few men were, and their crimes were grave.

On the path to the river, Eagle Owl foraged for berries, hoping to appear strong when his mother came, for she would surely visit him. Would she dare to bring smoked fish? His stomach growled like a hungry cub. Why could he not teach it to behave as the old priest did? Namontack went for days without eating when ceremony required a fast. What magic went into such power of denial?

The early morning cooking fires of others sent smoke downwind, toward the tangled undergrowth and a strawberry patch Eagle Owl picked clean of fruit, digging in the dirt for fallen berries. He recalled the first time he saw the skinny English boy who had gotten him into so much trouble. The boy picked slowly, like an old woman; Eagle Owl smiled. The young intruders knew nothing of foraging or wrestling or healing. Yet he had courage, that pale sapling of a boy, and he understood the vision that had cost Eagle Owl so dearly.

Eagle Owl listened for the calls of the people. Some Algonkians lived just outside the palisades of the fort built by the English. They traded with the intruders and worked for them; in return, they got clothes, tobacco, and rum. The drink made the men crazy, and many had spent nights retching inside the stockade. Anger against the intruders, who should not take advantage of people, grew with every sunrise and sunset. Eagle Owl feared conflict.

At his home village, he knew by the light, children now scurried to build fires; the women urged them to hurry. The sun was rising. He touched the cross given him by the English boy. It was smooth as a rock polished by the river but weighed little; the sun glinted off it as though it were a blade. He smiled. He had given in return the nugget so prized by the English, gold in color but false at its core, like an apple rotting from within. Why did the English like gold so much? The nugget was too small to make into anything, even a ring.

He heard someone coming and crouched behind a bush covered in sweet wilting honeysuckle. Perhaps it was Grey Hawk, come to mock and torment him. Grey Hawk could track a wild turkey on a moonless night. Eagle Owl hid, digging his feet into the soft wet earth. Dust from the leaves tickled his nose but he dared not sneeze.

It was Great Eagle. His father had crossed the river to give his exiled son one last look, his face composed in sorrow before turning to leave. Eagle Owl knew that the werowance had made noise so that his son would hear him and see the pain in his eyes. His father's ploy worked; tears filled his eyes, and he would have wept but for his pride. His father walked away with a heavy step and disappeared into the pines and tangled undergrowth leading to the river.

He set about improving his house, gathering saplings
to bend for the support poles and peeling the bark for the
roof and walls. He gathered rush and reeds at the riverside
and made a mat to cover the hole through which he could
comfortably enter and leave. Inside the pouch hanging by
the flap, he found and held the treasures he had shown the
English boy: they seemed so much foolishness now, as he
sat alone miles from his village, across the river from his
mother and sisters, and too near the English, whom his father had warned him to ignore. He could not help feeling
that the dream granted him was a test of his faith and
courage and that he would be shown to be right, if he could
live that long. What of the old priest's brother held inside
the English fort? He must free him, but how?

🔻 🔻 🔻

That night, in a soft hissing drizzle, Eagle Owl paddled
across the wide river and made his way home. He wanted
to see his mother, to ask her help and forgiveness, and to
ask her advice. The woods and streams were alive with the
raucous bragging of bullfrogs and the chirruping of crickets seeking mates. An owl—perhaps the one that gave him
his name—whooed overhead and stared at Eagle Owl as he
passed, recognizing him. The owl turned its head sharply;
it heard something. Eagle Owl froze and listened. Someone
was coming. He crouched by the path, hidden by the trunk
of a fallen oak.

His younger cousin walked the path holding a bundle
in his arms. Eagle Owl sprung out, and the boy dropped
the bundle, screaming. His hands jumped to his face.

Eagle Owl laughed and hugged him, but the boy
punched and kicked, furious at the deception. Eagle Owl
dodged the kicks and let the punches fall; they did not hurt
him. Later, they spoke of his mother and sisters as Eagle
Owl unwrapped the leather bundle. Inside were moccasins,
leggings, dried smoked fish wrapped in reeds, flat corn
bread, arrowheads, and a skin to cover with while sleeping. Eagle Owl sent his cousin home after learning that his

father had told the boy how to find him and had allowed his mother to send him the bundle.

Eagle Owl watched the agile boy go without waving or saying goodbye. He vowed to live as holy men do, alone, in prayer and work. Yet the image of Quiet Lark doing cartwheels through the village entered his mind, and he had to smile, thinking of her. He missed them all so much. What move would Grey Hawk make while he was gone?

🏹 🏹 🏹

His mother awoke without making a sound. Oholasc knew that her son was there before he touched her arm. She motioned for silence and crept with him out the door and to the edge of the woods, outside the palisades that marked their village. The rain fell steadily now, silencing the crickets and the bellowing bullfrogs. His mother's long hair was straight and smelled of bear oil and the fire.

"Your father will be angry," she told him, squeezing his arm.

Eagle Owl nodded. "If he learns—"

"He knows. Heed your father. In time, you will be taken back. Quiet Lark will not fly away. You are the chief's son. Act like one!"

Eagle Owl was surprised by his mother's stern words. He started to protest—he was lonely and just a boy—when he realized that living on his own was something he had wanted to do for years. He kept quiet. The rain drenched them.

"Go now, wet fool! You have what you need." She touched his forehead and sent him away.

He ran toward the river with her smell and touch upon him like a blessing. He would survive.

In the darkness, he took the wrong path and had to retrace his steps. The canoe trip across the river left him cold and wet, and so weary he could barely keep his eyes open. He found his house to be dark and chilly. The fire had gone out and it was too wet to make a new one. He lay huddled and miserable in a skin, praying to the gods for forgiveness and for the chance to prove himself worthy of a proud name. Sleep crept up on him like an enemy and found him.

❧   ❧   ❧

Days and nights passed quickly, in a blur of trapping, foraging, and gathering firewood. Eagle Owl kept the fire burning inside his house and the mildew disappeared. He fished and hunted, bringing home deer, raccoon, and rabbit. He skinned and preserved the hides as his mother had done, eating everything else. Hearts and livers were a delicacy and gave one strength and endurance. He prayed for forgiveness every morning and night and bathed in the river with each rising of the sun, never seeing another Algonkian from his village. Several worked in the English village, and he watched them saunter off to the fields with their masters in front. He felt shame for them. They trailed behind their masters like dogs. Eagle Owl withdrew to his house when the planters and their servants walked to and from the ripening tobacco fields. The odd, round sounds of their chatter disturbed the peace he was building within himself.

He had no more dreams of the English. His visions were of his family laughing, telling tall hunting tales around the fire, the men smoking green tobacco and the women hiding their mouths, laughing too. The children dashed around them in circles, chasing each other, before running outside into the sunshine. In his dreams, the sun shone brightly. But when he awoke, the mornings were hazy and grey, and the days often shattered by thunderstorms. Once lightning struck a tree so close that he heard a great crash and smelled the fire and the smoke. When he ran out to see, the tree had fallen just twenty feet away and lay sizzling in the rain, smoking like a giant's pipe. The sight made him laugh, and he feared the storms no more.

One morning two weeks after his banishment, Eagle Owl was bathing in the river when his father suddenly appeared in a canoe, perhaps a half-mile away. His father raised one arm: come, he meant. Come home. Eagle Owl whooped and ran to his house, gathering his things. He brought the hides and furs, his weapons and tools. He paddled home so fast, the otters and the beavers could not keep up. His wake swirled with silvery light, and just as in his dreams, the sun shone hot and bright, burning off the morning haze. The woods were sweet with honeysuckle and ripe huckleberries. He ran past the palisades and into his family's yehawkin. His sisters danced and sang as his mother held him tight, so close he could smell nothing but her and the fire.

"Where is father?" he asked. The children whooped and sang; he had to shout to be heard above them.

"Fishing. You are to stay here until he returns."

Eagle Owl did not protest. As his mother fed him, he told the children stories of ghosts and spirits haunting the woods, of headless bears with teeth in their paws, and of owls that spoke, demanding beads or they would pluck a boy's eyes out. The children were frightened. Their mother hushed him with more trout and corn and squash and flat baked cornbread, stuffing Eagle Owl. His little sisters fell over him again and again, as if he would never be free of their touch.

When his father returned with a basket of fish to be cleaned and smoked, he motioned Eagle Owl to follow him outside. Their mother held the other children inside and hushed them.

"You will fish and hunt with Grey Hawk and the other boys."

"I want to stay with the priest."

"No. You are to be a hunter, and soon, a warrior."

Eagle Owl kept quiet. The weeks by himself had taught him the value of silence. He would wait until his father relented. He yearned to be a priest, to heal and read signs and portents in the sky, and to see what was yet to happen. But for now, he would heed his father and do what he must as best he could.

🦅   🦅   🦅

The deer raised his head and froze. The wind had shifted; the animal had smelled them. Grey Hawk, who wore a buck's head and antlers, glared at him: shoot! Eagle Owl slowly raised the bow, watching the buck from the side of his eye, and took aim. The buck was poised to run but held his ground. As Eagle Owl held the bow with its tension at the greatest, his arm shook and he released the arrow. The buck bolted; the arrow hit him in the rump, and he leapt high over a log, bounding away. Grey Hawk jumped to his feet just twenty feet in front of the buck, which turned to flee. Too late; his arrow pierced the deer's eye, and the buck fell dead to the ground. The other boys flocked around Grey Hawk, slapping him on the back. Eagle Owl waved but kept his distance. He heard them whispering about him, the "dreamer of great dreams" who could no longer kill a buck with one arrow. He was an outsider now, until he did something to regain the trust of his fellows. But what could he do? They hunted and fished together; there was no time for heroics. They were at peace with the other Powhatan tribes and rarely saw the intruders, except canoeing past them in the river. An uneasy quiet endured between the two peoples.

Once at night, Eagle Owl overheard his father talking quietly with an Algonkian from another village, a son of the great chief Opechancanough. The two men sounded tense and uncertain, and they seemed to argue, but their speech was so soft and low, he could not be sure. He dared not ask his father.

At the temple the next day, Eagle Owl approached the priest but was rebuffed. "Go away!" the old man told him, squinting as if he could not bear to look directly upon the young hunter. He was smoking green tobacco and studying the smoke, or just thinking—Eagle Owl could not be sure. A west wind ushered him out of the temple, no doubt the old priest's doing.

Eagle Owl pleaded and prayed and fasted, passing more than one night alone, in and out of the sweat lodge, dashing to the river when the heat was about to boil his brains and sear his skin, but no more visions came to him, just a loneliness and an unease. He felt as though the earth might shake him loose and send him hurtling into the heavens at any moment.

The next time he went to the temple to bring firewood and venison to Namontack, the priest tore at the cross around the boy's neck, but Eagle Owl would not let him have it. "It is mine!" he protested, running away. The priest called down a curse upon him, and Eagle Owl fell in a gopher hole and sprained his ankle. He could not jump or run for a week.

Eagle Owl now slept in the family home with his mother, sisters, and the other members of her family. His father rarely spoke to him except to correct some mistake: "Put the bow there. Did you dry the strings? Why so few fish: are the waters too cold for you?" His displeasure with his only son was clear, and there was talk in the village that Great Eagle would soon wed another maiden, to have more worthy sons by her.

But for his mother and the comfort of Quiet Lark, who dared to smile at him and playfully tossed ripe huckleberries at him, Eagle Owl had never felt so alone and unloved. He might not be a priest at all. Hunting and fishing were not enough for him; he longed to lead and guide and foresee, and if he were not allowed to develop those powers, he feared that he might be forced to live alone in the woods across the river forever, a scorned hermit, a man without a people.

He slept raggedly, awakening to every acorn falling in the woods outside the yehawkin, and he dreamed no more.

Chapter Seven

THE POWER OF GOLD

After Thomas's miraculous escape, he was hailed as a boy to watch—until he spoke up about his Indian friend, a boy with a vision of uniting the two races. Thomas was shunned, even by Priscilla Powell, who now took in laundry from two of the kinder and more forgiving families. His father said little once he returned, but forced a promise out of Thomas: he would never run away again into the woods, not alone. Thomas swore upon his mother's grave and knew that this was one oath he had to keep, at the peril of his soul. His father put him to work with a vengeance, treating him little better than a servant, for in the summer there was too much work and too few hands.

The corn was high, but the dry July earth drank too much water. A thunderstorm rolled in most afternoons and helped with the watering chore, but the damage done by the winds and driving rain made matters worse. Thomas had to replant some corn when the fragile stalks were toppled in the wind and snapped like the mast of a ship caught in a storm at sea. He lamented the care he had to give the garden behind their cottage. His mother had done the work without complaint, but Thomas had dreams—he had held a gold nugget in his hand. His father shooed him away and called gold fever a madness, threatening to throw the nugget down the village well. When she spoke to him, after dark, in hushed whispers, Priscilla thought the gold nugget pretty in the firelight but laughed when he suggested they wed and run off to the mountains in search of more gold. She too called him mad, although she laughed when she said it. Thomas was weary of being thought a fool and a child. He would show her, and soon, that he was neither a fool nor a madman.

The chickens clucked and pecked for grains and wandered off; he was forever scurrying after them, wasting precious time tending dumb fowl who ought to be plucked and roasted and devoured. His stomach growled for meat, but he and his father lived on squash, corn, bread, and the occasional wild turkey Charles shot on the way to or from the tobacco fields. Sometimes his father traded labor for fish and fowl, but too often to suit Thomas, their dinner was cold and unsatisfying. He hid his complaints, for the back of his father's hand was quick and hard, and Thomas was only now beginning to look like himself, with his cheek no longer swollen and both eyes clear and blue. Every so often, out of the blue, the buzzing in his ear returned and he was half-deaf, a calamity he could never convince his father of.

"You're not half-deaf," his father insisted, eyeing him with distrust, "you're whole-lazy."

♣ ♣ ♣

The last week in July, the Collier boy, Samuel, just three, ate a wild mushroom, convulsed, and died in his mother's arms. Thomas felt little of the family's pain. Death was all too common. Two nights later, a small band of savages raided the company stores in the dead of night, carrying off meal and drink. They moved without making a sound, like spirits of the dead, and spooked the village from one rampart to the other. The widow Powell was unseen for weeks, although Priscilla walked every day to the well and was watched over by Matthew Garret, who dared any man to make a comment against her. Thomas continued to take her firewood and food in the early hours of the morning, when all but the haunted slept, but he rarely saw Priscilla and missed her voice and face and sparkling eyes. Only Matthew, whose fists were hard and whose mother was Christian to the core, dared to visit the witch's daughter in daylight, bringing flowers and meal and fowl. The two of them talked for hours while Thomas seethed.

The Burgess laughed when Thomas suggested the old Indian held in the stockade be released; his father whipped him again when he heard about it, and forced him to work all day in the tobacco fields with only water to drink and a crust of bread to eat. Thomas learned to keep quiet. If patience was a virtue, he was becoming too virtuous for his own good. He had no one to talk to and carried on long conversations with Priscilla in his head, but when he saw her, his tongue stiffened and swelled and he only nodded or wished her "good day," praying her mother would not step forward with flames darting from her tongue. Matthew always seemed to linger nearby, cracking his knuckles, praying for the chance to knock Thomas cold in a fair fight. Thomas ran away each time Matthew approached, though he cursed the cowardice that ran through his blood like a bad humor.

Most days, Thomas had to help his father in the fields, mending the hog fences they had built to keep wild pigs out of the tobacco fields. The hogs rooted and stomped the tobacco leaf into ruin. Shouting did no good; Thomas quickly learned that you had to thump the pig on the flank to get his attention and crack him on the head with a shovel to persuade him to move. But for Matthew Garret, a rooting pig was the most hard-headed beast in the New World, by Thomas's reckoning.

Hot and weary and bone-tired, Thomas walked at a pace more suited to an old man suffering the gout. The long walk to the village well was time wasted, when he could be scouting for gold in the streams or trying to find a good map of the mountains, if he only had a horse or a partner or enough tobacco to buy one or the other. Before his thrashing at the last Court Day, he had overheard two adventurers planning an expedition to the west, two men new to the village and just off-ship from England in May. They had seen enough hard work and tasted enough dust to know that living within the high walls of Jamestown was not for them. Thomas vowed to catch the men alone; he knew where they slept, in the house of the cobbler, Harris, behind the Powell cottage.

Thomas trudged farther down the dusty lane. Puddles lingered in the shadows from the pounding rain of two days ago, when a third of his corn stalks had fallen. He cursed the cloudy heavens, then retracted the curse. What if God heard him and ignored the retraction? Could God be arbitrary? Ask Job of Old Testament fame, his father would say: He afflicted the man with boils, poverty, and sorrow just to see if he would curse the Almighty. What were Thomas's woes compared to those of a man so sorely tested?

Thomas came to the lane between the cottages just inside the east wall of the fort. He hurried past his cottage and made for Priscilla's house. The Powell cottage tilted; the roof leaked from the last storm. Neither woman could be heard as he passed. He was relieved and crept past their withered garden like a thief. His eye had healed, his ear no longer rang; he yearned to remain whole and well, if possible. If that meant avoiding Priscilla Powell, who scorned him for that bullhead Matthew Garret, so be it. She would open her eyes one day soon and see what a fool she was.

A blackbird perched upon the fence behind the small garden plot Priscilla once kept free of weeds; the bird squawked at Thomas. He shivered and hurried past the Powell women's cottage, ashamed at his fear. More than one village gossip believed that the widow could turn herself into a crow at will, to spy on her neighbors and eat their corn on the stalk. Thomas scoffed at such a notion, but he did keep an eye out for an oriole that sang a distinctive three-note song of alarm.

He heard the raised voices of two men arguing twenty feet before he reached the open doorway of the cobbler's cottage. Harris's three-sided workshop stood just to the west, and there stood Mister Harris, hammering on the bottom of a boot, working as if deaf to the ruckus. Thomas froze and waited, hoping the argument would soon dissolve, like the midsummer morning haze. He could not help listening and glancing around, saw no one else. Most men were in the fields with their servants. The women and children of Jamestown were too busy tending their gardens, mending clothing, cooking, and cleaning to pay attention to an argument between two strangers. Thomas heard every word.

"It's a hundred miles or my name's Old Scratch!" His voice was thick and slurred, as if he had been drinking rum. Thomas was puzzled. How did the man expect to find gold with his head fogged by drink?

"If the mountains are that far, we're dead men," the other adventurer reasoned. "Without a horse—"

"No horses, you jackanape! They eat too much and can't be trusted. A horse isn't worth a cow tail."

In a moment of quiet, Thomas approached the cottage, which had a fireplace built into the wall and two windows. Flies buzzed everywhere. At the doorway the odor of strong drink hit Thomas in the face. Despite his fear, he stepped into the shadow of the doorway.

"Good day?"

A chair tilted and fell, spilling a heavyset man onto the floor. His partner laughed "Hee-hee-hee!", covering his mouth. On the table before him lay a folded brown map, which the man snatched and hid in his shirt.

"Help me up, boy! I am infirm."

Thomas scurried to help the man, who was solid and stocky and much too heavy to move. He looked helplessly to the other fellow, who shook with merriment, waving Thomas back. The man who had hidden the map was leaner and handsome but had not shaved in days, and his eyes were so deepset, he appeared to have none. "Let him lie there like a turtle that can't right himself!"

"Get me up, boy!" the husky man insisted, raising a hand. He wore the rough shirt and linen trousers of a working man, but his hand was smooth and plump, like a lady's. Thomas struggled but could not lift him. The man rolled over and got to his feet after a struggle. "What of it, boy? What's your business?"

Thomas took a breath. The sharp odor of rum almost stung his eyes. He saw a bottle on the table between them and two stone mugs. "I want to go with you, to find gold." The men began to laugh, giggling like children. They made faces at each other and choked with good humor. Thomas took out the nugget given him by the Powhatan boy. The men suddenly hushed. "I got this from a savage," Thomas explained. "He says it came from the mountains. I want to find more. Can I go with you? I can cook and I won't complain."

The lean fellow with no eyes introduced them. "I'm Willis, Tillman's the pig in the corner. No, you can't go. Your mother'd kill us—"

"My mother is dead." The words came out so quickly, he could not stifle them. Before the men could speak, a tear welled in his eye, and he wiped it away, biting his lip. "My father says I can go," he added, lying. "I am a free man."

Willis raised an eyebrow. "Your father's not got a say in it, boy. We sailed here together, me and Tillman, from London. We got dreams. Half the men here in bondage to another. They work six days a week for another man and got one day to call their own and what do they do? Work! That ain't for me nor my friend here. We ain't corn growers and tobac smokers: we got ideas! We also got no room for you or nothin' else, unless we can eat you or trade you to the savages for safe passage to the gold fields. What do you taste like gutted and boiled?"

Thomas gulped. Willis laughed. His teeth were yellow and stained brown by tobacco, which he spat onto the dirt floor in a liquid ball of dark, foul-smelling scum. "We don't need you, boy. I like your talk, though. If we strike a vein of gold wide as the James River and come back wealthy as good King James, I'll hire you to oversee my Virginia estate."

Tillman cackled like a hen, a high-pitched laugh for such a hearty man. He reached for the bottle. "Deal?"

Thomas could not agree. For the first time, he had spoken of his mother's death. His heart flew out his mouth when he spoke, and he felt hollow, as if the next stiff west wind might carry him away, far out to sea, where he would be lost forever, adrift and homeless. The men frightened him; their drinking in the morning was wrong, he knew. He excused himself and ran out of the cottage into the hot sunlight; their laughter trailed him for a moment, but he outran it.

Taking a roundabout route to avoid passing the Powell cottage, Thomas passed the jail and heard a hubbub. Someone called for the minister, never a good sign. Thomas elbowed his way in front of a crowd of women and boys and found prone before them on the ground the old Indian, "the old thief," they called him. He lay still and pale.

"Dead," a woman said. "May God have mercy upon the heathen's soul, if he has one."

"The devil take him!" a boy cried.

Thomas was relieved not to see Matthew Garret about. Matthew brooked no argument and would surely call for the man's body to be dumped into the trenches outside the gates like waste. No one knew what to do with the savage. Burial was out of the question. Someone volunteered to run to Governor Wyatt's residence and ask him; the others agreed. Thomas turned back to the dead man. Besides his mother, he had never seen a dead person so close before. At sea, many people perished, but they died in darkness and were cast into the sea in shrouds. Their appearance was a mystery.

The old Powhatan looked to be carved of wood, made by a great woodworker. His jawline was sharp, his cheekbones pronounced and perfectly round. In an untamed way, the leathery old man was handsome, like a sketch of the false Greek gods Thomas had once spied in a book back home in England.

With the others talking and looking the other way, awaiting the Governor's arrival, Thomas suddenly jumped. The savage beckoned to him with his eyes. Hesitant, shaking, Thomas took a step closer and bent over the man. The old savage they all believed to be dead opened his mouth—or his mouth simply fell open—and out flew a white dove. Jumping back, Thomas blinked, and it was gone. Sorcery! The old man is a magic man, a sorcerer, he realized. The old man's mouth had no teeth; his tongue was pale and thick. Shaken, Thomas withdrew, wondering how such tricks were accomplished. No one else had seen the dove. The others murmured and waited, eager to dispose of the body, ignorant of who the man was and what he might yet do to all of them. Where had the dove gone? He looked high in the trees but could not see it. The man he was to be traded for was dead. How would the Powhatans feel now? What would they do? He should have stayed their prisoner and come home when the Berry Thief's father allowed it. Such a trade was just. Now the Powhatans had another reason to hate the English, and Thomas was the reason. He had failed his friend; he had failed himself.

After the fear sent up by the old sorcerer rose and fell, a rush of inward pain attacked Thomas. There was too much death in this land, he lamented. Unlike the Israelites of old, he and his father and all the other planters and artisans and gentlemen were not the chosen people of God. Good King James had sent them, true, but he was no God and had made other mistakes. A tear rose and fell down his cheek. Thomas turned away, acting as if a piece of dust had caught in his eye. He hurried home and buried his face in his mother's pillow, weeping like a child, no longer able to smell his mother's sweet scent on the stuffed pillow.

That evening when his father returned, he washed away the tears and told him nothing of the adventurers Willis and Tillman. His short replies brought nothing but a stern, questioning look from his father, who inquired no further into the happenings of Thomas's day. Thomas wished he had an ally but knew that he was alone and could expect no help from anyone, save the Berry Thief. He wondered if the young savage had also been thrashed by his father.

"See that you keep away from the witch and her daughter," his father warned yet again, washing the dust and clay off his face and arms before supper. He was a silly sight—pale neck and shoulders, then arms so red he might be a heathen. Despite his gloom and fear, Thomas had to smile. He told his father about the dead savage, leaving out the part about the dove, and his father did a surprising thing: he took Thomas's head in his strong hand and kissed his son on the crown of his noggin, as though he were a child.

"Son, one day the light will dawn on the savages that we are not leaving, and on that day, there will be hell to pay up and down the river, mark my words." Thomas inquired and his father explained. "I work alongside savages and I tell you, I understand not one whit of how they think. No white man does. They are a mystery, and a mystery is dangerous. They can thank you one day and slit your throat the next, or so say them that knows the Indians best."

"What about Pocahontas?"

His father grinned. "You heard that story too? Did your mother tell you?" Thomas nodded. She had told him the tale one night before his father returned from the fields. "It may be true, but my guess is she had other reasons for saving that scoundrel. The Indians wanted guns and powder and trinkets. Smith gave them all freely, for corn and game. If she saved him, the big chief Powhatan let it be so."

"Mother said they could be trusted and should be educated, like us."

"Your mother was too kind ..."

They spoke no more and ate in silence. Thomas fell asleep in the heat and dozed fitfully, dreaming of the rain back home in England, and the cool cloudy days of summer, and of his mother's smile and touch, a healing touch he would never feel again this side of heaven.

Thomas heard the next morning that a delegation of three men had taken the dead savage to his folk across the James River, and all were treated with solemnity. There were no threats but for the young Indians, who waved bows and knives at them, but the trio arrived home safely. For that, they all gave thanks on Sunday, at the chapel.

🔥   🔥   🔥

Autumn crept in kindly, like an old English aunt come to visit, bringing bright colors and delightful cool and sunny weather that raised the spirits of all Jamestowners, young and old. Gold leaf tobacco hung heavy and yellow-spotted on thick green stalks. After being cut, the leaves were laid to dry in the sun for two or three days, then dried and heated in hot-house barns for half of October, curing and sweetening. Too much rain, too little sun, a fire too hot, and the tobacco was ruined, and so was the man who grew it. The days were long and tense, and Thomas found his father to be even more remote than ever before.

❧   ❧   ❧

Like the Indians, the women and children of Jamestown gathered hickory nuts, acorns, chestnuts, and walnuts while the tobacco harvest went on. They stored the hard nuts in large barrels in the company storehouse, near the chapel. In November, God and the prevailing winds willing, the ships from England would arrive with linen and tools, and the men of Jamestown would pile their holds high with the hogshead barrels of the bright-leaf tobacco that was almost their god. The English ships were sixty-foot long, eighty-ton beauties that everyone greeted at the docks with a whoop and a holler.

❧   ❧   ❧

The ships came just before the first great storm of the season, two tall pinnaces with white canvas sails billowing in the stiff breeze. The passengers were pale men, ill and weak. Most were tended by the surgeon, then found room and board with families who wanted the company as much as they needed the few shillings paid them for shelter and two meals a day. Once the new Comers had disembarked and their trunks were hurriedly tossed off the ships, fifty-pound hogshead barrels rolled endlessly toward the ships. Men calculated and squabbled and noted profits and costs in page after page of entry journals. Near-fortunes were made by the larger growers, men who owned more than fifty acres and had a score of servants working for them. Gentleman Martin, who owned one hundred acres of prime black earth just fifteen miles downriver from Jamestown, was said to be so wealthy he might buy himself the governorship, if he so desired. He was said to be building a grand manor house, a home so majestic that men who saw it swore it had been brought brick by brick from England and reassembled on the banks of the great river.

Most men profited, but not greatly; Thomas's father was one. He was pleased but not overjoyed. His dreams of wealth were as fleeting as the warm sun, which fled the first day in November. The Indians spoke of the winter wind as "the Hawk," and soon the English knew why. The wind bit at them and chilled them. No coat was warm enough, and their mean cottages whistled and moaned with a frigid northerly wind.

Early in November, during the curing of the harvest, the minister preached a sermon against pride and obsession, scolding the men who worshipped the tobacco leaf as if it were more than a weed to be smoked. He cautioned them against ignoring man's other needs, spiritual and physical. The talk made sense to Thomas, although the substitution of "gold" for "tobacco" would have disturbed him greatly. In a land where tobacco was green gold and every man dreamed of a bigger crop next year and the next, the minister's words rang hollow, and were widely ignored.

Willis and Tillman, who had rejected Thomas's offer of partnership, had left late in August for the mountains, when the haze and the heat were at their cruelest. No word had been received from them in the three months since. The fall rains were relentless, and in the middle of November, water crept up into the floors of their cottages. Sweeping it out became a battle of bucket and muscle. Straw rotted, hay spoiled; the animals moaned and sickened and died, weary as people of the cloudy wet days and chilling nights. Tobacco that had not yet been barreled and loaded aboard ship was ruined. Fevers ran through the village with abandon, and it seemed that everyone had sniffles and coughs, all but the Powell woman and her daughter, who though rarely seen in the daylight were said to creep about at night on cat's feet to steal food and chickens from neighbors. There was talk of another dunking, but a six-inch deep snowfall in mid-November put an end to idle chatter.

❧　❧　❧

In winter, survival was a challenge. Freezing to death was a miserable way to end one's days on earth; ice and freezing cold were relentless. Snow piled a foot deep on their roofs. The cannons slumbered under the snow. The geese had flown south, and even wild turkeys were scarce. Hares were few and hard to trap in the ice and snow, and sometimes men who went out alone into the woods in search of deer never returned.

At least one night a week, Thomas crept from his bed and out the door, skulking down the lane to the Powell cottage. If both women were asleep, he left the firewood that filled his arms by the door and crept back home. Often Priscilla heard him and arose, wrapping herself in a tattered gown, and she gave him herbs and salves for his cracked hands and to cure coughs. They worked. Once, as she crushed and mixed leaves and herbs in a small vial, Thomas overheard the widow Powell rambling, predicting a tragedy in the spring, "when the wild dogwoods bloom." She sounded old and quaky, weak and crazed. She prattled on about newly purchased pigs, "which must be backed into a pen or they will die." He had never heard such nonsense, and the hairs on his neck stood at attention. He fought the urge to run home and never return to their soggy, damp, miserable cottage.

The widow said more: "Anyone born in the first three days of the new year will lead a short and an unhappy life!" She chattered further, predicting who would die, and when. Thomas shivered and almost wished her dead and gone. If she were not a witch, she was mad, and that was frightening enough.

Thomas dreamed more and more of gold in the mountains and less of Priscilla's hair and eyes. When he asked her about the pink-eyed albino piglet, she told him coldly that "Little Thomas" had died, and they ate him. He looked about their cottage and never saw food, yet they lived. On what? As the winter went on, he brought them bread and cheese and winter squash, and when he could take them without his father's notice, smoked turkey and fish. Priscilla rarely thanked him and seemed distant, as if the pale cast to her face and the faraway look in her blue eyes were an indication that she might float away to another world up in the clouds and never look down again. She grew paler and leaner by the week and began to look more like a spirit than a girl to Thomas, who still yearned for her attention, although he had no intention of battling Matthew for the privilege of being spited and confused by her. When he was rich, he would find a pretty gentlewoman whose mother was dead and buried and marry her.

One night after a chilling rain, with the moon on the wane and the lane between the houses lost in shadow, Thomas was caught by the widow Powell as he lay stacked firewood at their door.

"Listen," she told him, her voice raspy and deep as a man's, "and you shall be the only farmer in the village to prosper. Know the moon, heed the moon, and you will prosper." Her hand on his arm was sharp as an eagle's talon. Her breath in his face reeked of garlic. "Plant herbs, garlic, and radishes in a new moon, but beware the setting goose that births blind goslings. In a waxing moon, sow grain but spare the hogs you might have slaughtered, for they will swell and grow foul in the barrel. A slaughtered cow yields the sweetest meat in the full moon, and a calf weaned will become a good milking cow. Cut and split timber and gather fruit in a waning moon; horses born in a waning moon will be weak, and a slaughtered pig will yield dry tough meat." She nodded once, having had her say, and walked back into the cottage, leaving no footprints behind her. Thomas shivered and ran home in a fever of fear. How could she remember so much nonsense and superstition? Was there room in the widow's head for a word of truth? He longed to shout at her, "I am no farmer!" but thought better of it and kept his silence. He vowed to beware of Priscilla until her mother was buried, but his heart fluttered when she spoke, for she was the only young beauty in the village.

On Christmas Eve, they stayed inside, huddling around the fire and sipping punch. Charles Spencer told his son of the old wives' tale, how dumb beasts acquired the power of speech on Christmas Eve but lost it at dawn on Christmas Day. Thomas listened closely to the lowing and cackling from the barn, but it sounded like no speech he had heard. What would he ask of the cow—how's the hay? He thought about the Berry Thief, his Indian friend, and wondered what he was doing that cold clear night. Had he too surrendered the dream? Was he lonely and miserable as well?

In late December, after a dismal Christmas feast of cold pudding and buttered bread, Thomas was met by Matthew in the lane by the Powell cottage. The wind was frigid and blew bits of ice and dry snow into their eyes and faces. Thomas shivered; his coat was flimsy, and without a blanket and a fire, he was always cold. Matthew stuck a finger in his chest.

"Priscilla will wed me in the spring," he said. His face was dirty and florid. What had he been doing to have worked up a sweat in the cold, Thomas wondered.

"We shall see," Thomas was bold enough to say, and Matthew cursed him as he strode home.

"She is mine!" Matthew shouted above the wind. He sounded desperate. "I'll break you in two!"

Thomas was so miserable and cold and wet that thoughts of love vanished. Perhaps Priscilla Powell, like the dogwood trees and the gold of the western mountains, was best dreamt-about and desired in the spring. He resolved to pity her no more and to work upon his own happiness and comfort. The hawk-wind blowing down from the mountains bit at his face and hands. He had not seen an Indian in weeks. He was hungry all the time and so lonely, he took to addressing the chickens as he might younger siblings, telling them his dreams. They clucked encouragement and fought over the corn. He dreamed of plucking and stewing one of them, here and now, but they needed the eggs.

❧ ❧ ❧

One frigid night late in January, Thomas struggled to carry
an armload of firewood to the Powell women. The wind bit
and howled; snowflakes danced in the twisting wind like
wild albino butterflies fallen from the heavens. There were
no stars; there was no moon, no sky. His breath froze on
his lips and his tongue cleaved to the roof of his mouth, as
Job's must have.

He came down the lane and froze. Lit by the glow of the
fire within her cottage stood Priscilla Powell and Matthew
Garret, locked in an embrace. Thomas dropped the wood
with a clatter. They started and faced him, their eyes full
and dark and guilty. Matthew said something in a sharp
tone but Thomas had already turned away. He ran home
and hid his face in his mother's pillow, cursing his eyes,
welcoming darkness and the blissful ignorance of the blind
and the dead.

❧ ❧ ❧

In mid-February, when the two-inch high tobacco seedlings
were tended like plants that yielded gold sovereigns, a
thaw swept through the village. Foot-long icicles crashed to
the ground and melted, rivers ran, and the snow dripped
into slush, and finally into inconsequence. Snowball fights
raged for the last time, and Thomas realized with mingled
pleasure and pain that the Powells would no longer need so
much wood; his heart and soul might be spared the sorrow
and pain of seeing Priscilla lose herself to that red-faced,
foolhardy devil Matthew. So be it; he had other dreams.

He was within ten feet of the cottage when he smelled
her and knew she was dead. He prayed it was the widow
alone and not Priscilla too. He ran into the house and saw
the old woman resting upon the bedstead, her head raised,
her face composed but dark and shiny as polished ma-
hogany wood, as natural and at peace as the leaf of a mag-
nolia lost in shadow. Priscilla appeared with a bucket of

water and as if Thomas were invisible, washed the face and arms of her mother as though to refresh and awaken her.

"She's dead, Priscilla," he said.

She ignored him. He ran to the preacher, who grimly nodded and sent him home.

🏹 🏹 🏹

The funeral was held on a sunny, cool day. You could taste spring in the air, the green minty breath of new life. The sweet stink of the river and the vitality of nature's verdant bounty filled the air. Only Thomas, his father, Matthew, his mother, and Priscilla attended the funeral, although John Capper and two of his friends observed, no doubt to be sure that the witch would remain dead and buried. The preacher read from the Psalms, number eighteen, verses sixteen and seventeen: "He drew me out of many waters." Someone guffawed; the preacher cast a stern glance in the direction of the laughter, and it quieted. "He delivered me from my strong enemy, and from them which hated me: for they were too strong for me."

Priscilla wept openly; Thomas was moved and surprised to find tears in his eyes. The Widow Powell was no doubt mad and pitiful but not hateful; if she was a witch, she had no choice, and no one had proved she had done any real harm. Crops withered and died from the heat and drought, not from the curses and ramblings of a lonely, eccentric, hungry old woman. This land was cruel enough without the invention of witches and demons.

After the service, the preacher invited Priscilla into the chapel for counsel. She emerged hours later and burst into tears at the sight of Matthew and Thomas, who waited in the cold chill for her.

"They're sending me downriver to serve a lady!" she cried. "For six years!" Her eyes were red, and her pale skin blotched, as if she had a mild case of the pox.

Matthew threatened to punch the Reverend silly, until he changed his mind; Priscilla begged him not to, and he swore to follow her "into the heart of savage country."

A man called out "Witch!" but was hushed by Matthew's charge. Thomas turned his back on the weird pair and hurried home with his father. There were tools to mend and seedlings to water. He could do no more for Priscilla Powell. She and Matthew were bound by desire and ill fortune. He prayed for them.

The next day Priscilla and her trunk were rowed downriver to Martin's Hundred, and that night Matthew disappeared. His mother came to Thomas for some word of the pigheaded boy, but he said nothing: they both knew where he had gone, and why. He had never seen Mrs. Garret so troubled. She scurried home with a red robe thrown over her shoulders like so much frozen blood. Thomas felt a chill fall over him when he prayed for the two of them that night, as if he would never see them again. Now that they were gone, he missed them. He had said goodbye to neither and wished he had. Goodbye and fare you well, friends, now and forever.

Chapter Eight

THE HUSKANAW

The dance began mid-morning, led by Great Eagle, the werowance; rattles were shaken, and drums beat a festive rhythm. Two men played flutes. The trees shook to the music, and forest animals scampered off. Dressed in their finest skins and feathers, the men danced four abreast, one circle of hunters moving in one direction and the other facing and dancing the opposite way. A squirrel paused in the branch of an oak to heave acorns in protest and chatter his disapproval. Children pointed at him and laughed. Vanquished, the squirrel jumped to the branch of another tree and escaped the noisy festivities.

Painted white by their elders, Eagle Owl, Grey Hawk, and six other boys of their age sat under an elm and watched their fathers and uncles and older brothers dance before them. As the men danced and sang, women laid out a feast in the woods beyond the palisades of the village. Everyone was there. Quiet Lark carried a reed tray piled high with venison; Eagle Owl caught her eye and held it for a moment in his intense stare. She blushed and kept her eyes on the heavy tray, careful not to drop it. Her teeth were white, and her back straight: she was a strong and beautiful young woman, and all the boys who were old enough to have such feelings wanted her for a wife. Eagle Owl was warmed by the thought of having her all to himself one day soon.

Around a fire, reed mats were set down for the men; before them lay smoked fish and sweetbreads. There was little corn left, and game was scarce. With the sun high overhead, everyone sat down to eat, and the men and boys ate and belched with appreciation. The women and girls ate too. For a while, when there was no music, the songs of the larks and wrens could be heard echoing through the trees. Soon the men stood, stretching and yawning, still hungry, and formed two circles. Two men picked up their drums, and the flutes twittered, and away flew the birds once again. The forest belonged to the people once more.

After noon, the dancing and chanting and music went on for hours without pause or rest. If a man grew tired and fell behind in the dance, one of the old priest's helpers ran forward and beat him with a bound bundle of reeds. Namontack had only to point, and a weary man was struck.

Into the center of the dancing, dizzying circles ran four men sporting black horns upon their heads; they held green boughs and howled like demons. Flinging away the boughs, the men ran into the woods and scaled a small tree effortlessly, where they clapped their hands and hissed. As Eagle Owl, Grey Hawk, and the other boys his age watched in fascination, the horned men jumped out of the small tree and tore it apart, limb by limb. Leaves and branches littered the forest floor. Sweating and huffing, the men fell back into the dance; the tree was dead. Now they were the tree.

When the dancers gasped for breath and some fell to the ground in exhaustion hours later, Eagle Owl and the other boys in white body paint were brought into the circle. The men danced around them and sang. Women and girls smiled and cheered them. The boys were led by older men, fighters and hunters, to an immense oak tree and forced to sit beneath it, in a semicircle. The older men made fierce sounds and shook their tomahawks at unseen demons in the deep woods, as if guarding the boys from harm. Eagle Owl and the other boys drew nearer to each other, their knees touching, but for Grey Hawk, who sat up straight and smirked, showing no fear. As Eagle Owl and the others watched, their guards formed two lines; between them came five older youths, young men who like Eagle Owl wanted to be priests and seers and healers. One by one, Eagle Owl and the other boys were led through the lane between the older men, who pretended to be furious at the "abduction" of the boys and beat them as they raced by. Eagle Owl was swatted about the face and neck by the stinging reeds before being hustled to safety in the shade of a tall pine at the far edge of the deep woods. When all the boys had gathered beneath the pine and seated themselves on a cushion of pine needles, the older men attacked the tree, tearing off branches that they set in their hair like wreaths. Scattered needles and pine cones lay everywhere. Again and again, the boys were forced to run the gauntlet between two lines of warriors, who beat them with reed switches. Eagle Owl understood that they had pretended to be abducted and released three times, and that something more was going to happen to him and the other boys before they would be considered to be men. All the while, women and girls wept openly and called out for their boys, some of them singing dirges and wailing as if their sons and brothers had died. Beside the wailing women lay dry wood, mats, skins, and dry brown moss, everything needed for a funeral.

With a cry of the old priest, the boys were led out of the clearing and deep into the woods, down a steep ravine. Eagle Owl could see little but leaves and branches; the undergrowth and vines and pine trees blocked his view. He struggled to keep up with the others, who were led across a rocky stream that ran through the bottom of the muddy ravine. They came to a small clearing, and a pond. In front of them stood Great Eagle, dressed in the feathers and hides of a werowance. They stopped and looked at him, awaiting his word. He motioned them forward, and through a gap in the berry bushes and tangled undergrowth lay another feast: bread and venison, baskets of fish, roasted quail and turkey. Encouraged by their werowance, the boys sat and ate until they could not move. To their delight, their families joined them, there was music once more, and the children danced until they could not catch their breaths.

Suddenly the older men produced the stinging reed whips and stood to form two lines. One final time, the boys ran between the older men and were beaten, yet they were not led away to the safety of an oak or a pine tree. Instead, Eagle Owl and the other boys were made to lie still and lifeless beneath a sycamore tree. The old priest made it clear to them that they were dead and would be mourned. The older men, hunters and fighters, danced around them and sang their praises. The men then sat around the boys, who lay still and quiet, with their eyes shut tight. The werowance ordered the others to light the dry wood, which had been built in a steeple. The fire rose and crackled, and the boys were said to be dead. Eagle Owl felt his heart slow: is this what death is like? He felt weary and sluggish and honored, all at once, and wished he could sleep, now, forever. His back and hands stung where he had been whipped; the air cooled the burn and the bite of the reeds.

The others were sent away by his father; he could hear their steps and their fading hushed conversation in the brush. Soon the children and women had gone, and only the men remained. The boys had been still and silent for so long and the feast had been so bountiful that more than one boy had fallen asleep. It was dusk, and in the deep woods, the sun had disappeared. The smell of wood smoke was sweet and strong. Darkness crept over them like the wings of a great beast.

🦅 🦅 🦅

Eagle Owl was roughly shaken and dragged to his feet in darkness. He caught a glimpse of the fire, and a rough cloth was thrown over his head and tied around his neck. He was blind and stumbled as he was carried away. When he cried out, someone thumped him with a club, once, hard. He imagined hearing his mother cry out for mercy but no one answered. He walked and was half-dragged away from the pond and the clearing, led through a gap in the pines, and pushed deep into the woods, far from the home fire and the warmth of his mother's house. Why? Who had taken him now? Wasn't the huskanaw and his coming into manhood complete? He was so weary and full of roast game and hominy that he could barely keep his footing.

The hood over his face was raised once; a strong hand stuffed bitter cooked roots into his mouth and forced him to chew them. They ran farther into the tangled undergrowth of the woods. It was dark. The bag was replaced, and he fought for each breath. He tripped and fell and was dragged until he found his footing; his shins ached, and his head throbbed. The night was moonless and cold; he shivered and prayed for shelter, for the bitter roots had made him dizzy and thinned his blood, which ran like cold mountain water in his veins. Where was his father?

He heard Grey Hawk call out, once, demanding to know who had seized him: a blow silenced him as well. How many were there? These were not English kidnappers; they were too quiet and sure of their way in the woods at night. A Monacan raid? Why take the boys? Monacans stole women. They had no use for boys. It made no sense to him. He could not think clearly; his head was full of spider webs, and his tongue grew thick and dry.

They stumbled farther, walking blindly; Eagle Owl fell once again and was dragged until he found his footing and stepped quickly, like a bat meandering through a cave whose every passageway and cranny he had memorized.

Finally they stopped. No one spoke, but he heard the hushed heavy breathing of men. Eagle Owl gasped for air; the leather sack allowed him little fresh air. If he panicked, he might die. The dizziness intensified; he spun around and fell to the earth, the cold moist beating earth, yet the spinning continued. He saw in the darkness of his mind a light spinning and weaving, and from it emerged a Great Hare who shared dominion over the world with the four winds, who were like gods without substance. The Hare created men and women, storing them in a great bag until he could feed them. The winds visited the Hare and asked to eat the men and women but were shamed and sent away. The Hare fashioned water and fish and land and a Great Deer to feed upon the land and to drink the water. Jealous, the four winds returned, killing the Great Deer with spears; the wind gods dressed and ate the carcass and disappeared again. Having observed the winds' actions, the Great Hare gathered all the hairs of the slain Great Deer and scattered them across the earth, uttering many powerful words and casting many charms, whereupon each hair became a deer. Finally, after driving away the Giant Cannibal Spirits, the Great Hare released the People, setting one man and one woman in one Country and another pair in a distant land. So began the World, so began the People.

The story came to Eagle Owl whole, as if composed of one word. After the vision fell away, Eagle Owl heard a hoarse but familiar voice. The village priest, Namontack! He was safe, he would be well.

The sack was torn from his face. He blinked once; an owl spoke to him, or was it a man dressed in owl feathers? He could not be sure. The owl sounded like the old healer. What trick was this? His sorcery was powerful!

They were gathered in a circle, he saw now, he and Grey Hawk and six others, all the village boys of thirteen summers or more. Squatting, they sat hunched over, fearful, cold, like young animals abandoned to the woods. Wild animals ran and flew at them, waving their claws and feathers; one of them spoke to Eagle Owl. It was a giant Eagle Owl, his beast, a bird of prey with great talons and eyes that saw clearly in the darkness. The story was the same as in his vision, how the World came to be, and where the People came from. The sound of his voice came in waves, like the water lapping the shores of the great river after a storm. He heard some words, others were lost and meaningless. A black cannibal spirit rushed at them, and the boys cowered and covered their heads. The spirit howled and danced menacingly at them before disappearing into the woods. Eagle Owl raised his head and dared to look: only the old priest sat with the boys. Namontack wore buckskins and bright body paint. His face was grim, his mouth small and tight. Eagle Owl wondered if he and the other boys had failed the test of manhood already. His heart beat fast, then slow; the beat of his blood rose and fell with a rhythm he had never known, as if a demon had inhabited his body and was using it for a purpose Eagle Owl could not discern. He shook with fright and cold and wished his mother were near, but hid his fear as best he could, praying for strength.

A faint grey light broke through the tops of the trees. The dawn was sickly, spooked by the cannibal spirits. The priest stood, took corn meal from a pouch at his waist and dropped it from his hand, forming a circle around himself. He found a half-dozen sharp sticks and lay them inside the circle of meal. "The world is flat and round, and we stand in the center of it," the priest said slowly, looking closely at each boy to see that he understood. The healer's voice was clear and strong. "The sticks represent the houses and canoes of the intruders, who do not belong." One by one, the healer removed the sticks from the inside the circle of meal and broke them in half, casting them away. The sticks made no sound as they fell in the woods.

The earth throbbed and beat below Eagle Owl's feet, as if the great earth-heart lived just below the dirt and grass upon which he sat. He grabbed onto something and held on, fearing he might spin free of the world to fly away into nothingness, forever. Whatever he had grabbed jerked free of him, and he heard a cry of pain and hoped that he had not broken another boy's arm in his fear and confusion.

Eagle Owl fell back, exhausted, his world spinning; powerful hands (claws?) caught him and pushed him upright and back into the wavering circle of boys, who moaned and cried out in wonder and fear. The huskanaw! Eagle Owl's mind cleared for a moment, and he recognized the ritual for what it was, that time when boys became men and cast away all that they had known and all that had sheltered and nourished them as boys. Mother, brothers, sisters, fathers—all gone now, left behind in the safety and the firelight of the village. They would return, but as men, and they would no longer live in their mothers' houses. They must have no memory of the coming weeks or they would be forced to endure the pain and separation and the hunger once more. This much and only this much did he know of the huskanaw.

A streak of pink lit the horizon. Eagle Owl blinked again and again, struggling to clear his vision. The pink line of light wavered and whirled impossibly. The roots! He had eaten jimsonweed. It made a man dance with the devils and fogged his mind. He knew enough now to sit still and to listen to the roar of his breathing and the rush of blood in his ears. The beat of his blood was a drum that drowned out all other sounds. Where were the morning birds, the larks and wrens, the rapacious jays, the cardinals? He heard nothing but the rhythm of his flesh, and when he opened his eyes again, the sun was high overhead and he was drenched with sweat.

Hours had passed, perhaps the better part of a day and more. Eagle Owl reached for a gourd of water but dropped it. His lips cracked and stuck together. His throat was choked with dust and weeds and tasted as if a dry, foul ivy had taken root there.

🪶   🪶   🪶

Drums pounded; he blinked and it was night. Stars swirled in the heavens. A man sang of Creation and the birth of the People. Stories rang around them, and demons dashed into the firelight only to disappear before he could fight them or run away. Hideous faces, fanged and leering, snarled inches from his face. Eagle Owl recoiled and hid, but hands unseen forced his head up. Demons danced into and through the fire, which licked at the tops of the trees and threatened to catch the stars on fire. Only Grey Hawk sat up straight and failed to hide his face from the demons. But his eyes betrayed doubt and fear, and in that, Eagle Owl took heart.

The chanting grew; more voices joined, unseen voices of men he must know but could not recognize. He was fed a liquid paste and a gourd of water. He ate and drank greedily, slurping like a beast.

Unexpectedly, the reassuring and kind face of Little Dove smiled at him; her head floated above the flames for a moment, smiled and vanished. He called out—or tried to— but she was gone. A blessing? Why was he not granted a vision of her daughter, Quiet Lark, whom he hoped to marry?

One day when the air was clear and the sun warm, the boys were not fed the jimsonweed. Free to roam the small haphazard village that was now their home, their senses returned to them with heightened power. They marveled at the hawk's cry in the still morning air high above them. A dove flew in their midst and spoke to them. He was the spirit of the magic man who had died in chains in the intruders' village.

"Heed my brother's words," the old priest ordered, but none of the boys understood the dove's speech. Namontack appeared stricken and sad, and he withdrew from them for a day and a night. Eagle Owl pounded the cold earth in frustration: the old man he had failed to free was speaking to him. Why was he unable to understand? He could see his breath in the air but failed to see what the dove would teach him.

A cool breeze refreshed them; cold springwater on their lips was the god's nectar. One boy had died in the night. He lay stiff and blue in the morning. The others gathered around him. The old healer chanted and sang and blessed his journey into the next world. He was carried away by two older men in deerskins.

That night, Eagle Owl was called into the bark house of the healer, who sat alone by the fire. The old man looked stern, weary, and old as the ancients.

"Tell me of your visions."

Eagle Owl swallowed hard. He was so hungry and weary, he could fall asleep in a hailstorm. "I have none."

"Tell me."

Eagle Owl began with his vision of Creation, as it had come to him in a vision, before the story was told aloud to the group. The old man nodded. Eagle Owl mentioned Little Dove's face, and the demons. "That is all I remember."

The old man nodded. "Good. Our god Okewas demands obedience." He sent Eagle Owl away.

Another night, as the boys huddled around a roaring fire, the priest told the story of the great chief who approached the intruders five or more autumns ago, bearing a bow and arrows in one hand and a smoking pipe in the other. The intruders chose neither. "They do not know their own hearts," the priest explained, spitting in the dust. "They bring disease and filth. They kill us with their uncleanliness. Famine and poxes follow them like brothers. They do not know their own hearts! They plant their houses and their tobacco on our land and call it their own. Can they be so ignorant? The land has been ours since the First Day, and it shall be ours until the Last Day."

The boys slept and shivered in hastily constructed bark houses; some wept for their mothers in the night. All of them cried out in hunger and thirst, for some days they were fed nothing, and without their weapons, they could not hunt. Some prayed for death to take them over the mountains.

In five weeks, after a shortened huskanaw that left them all weak and troubled, Eagle Owl, Grey Hawk, and the others returned to the village as men. Skin hung taut on their coppery faces, which were weathered and lined. The whites of their eyes were streaked with red. They all needed baths and a day in and out of the sweat lodge and the river. They walked with the light step of a hunter, and filled with the stories and songs of the People from long ago, they knew themselves to be men who would one day soon be warriors and priests. Their families greeted them with respect, as they greeted a hunter and a warrior, not as boys who had been chided or rebuked.

Eagle Owl thought his mother looked smaller, although her bearing was as straight and proud as before. There were dark rings under her eyes, circles of worry and sleeplessness. Yet she smiled and hugged him and whispered how proud she was to have him as her son. She wanted to feed him roast turkey and fish and hominy, but he held up his hand.

"I am too weary to eat." They both laughed, for Eagle

Owl had never before been too tired to eat. His mother
bowed and withdrew, and he fell asleep sitting up, resting
on a pile of skins near the door.

🦅 🦅 🦅

After the huskanaw, the younger boys no longer taunted
him, and no one mentioned his vision or his exile. He
rested in his mother's house and ate and slept for one day
before solemnly taking furs, weapons, and dried fish and
corn to Little Dove's house. He was distressed to discover
that Quiet Lark was not there. She now lived in a small
bark house at the edge of the village with her aunt and
mother until she emerged as a woman. Eagle Owl asked to
be married to her, and her father nodded, taking the gifts,
though he would have to speak with Little Dove later, and
gain her approval as well. Eagle Owl resolved to pass the
night in and out of the sweat lodge, alone with his
thoughts. As he paused in the opening to the house, he
heard her father eating the fish and hoped that when Quiet
Lark returned to her home, at least one of his gifts would
remain uneaten or undisturbed.

Stepping outside Little Dove's yehawkin, he was met by
Grey Hawk, who carried no weapons and challenged him
to a fight for the right to wed Quiet Lark. The sunlight
made them squint. No other boys had gathered to watch;
perhaps Grey Hawk had warned them off so he could use
all his wrestling tricks. Paying the young men no mind,
women and children scurried to and fro, from yehawkin to
the corn fields and to the stream for water. No one paid
any attention to them. The men were off fishing and hunting. Eagle Owl would have to talk his way out of this fight.

"A seat in the sweat lodge and a dunk in the river is
what we need," Eagle Owl said, hoping to jostle the taller,
stronger fighter out of his dark mood. He showed his teeth
in what he hoped was a friendly grin.

Grey Hawk spat at the ground before Eagle Owl. "You
are a man now, not an old woman. Fight me!"

Eagle Owl wondered what would happen if he lay face

down in the dirt and played dead. He feared that if he closed his eyes, he would fall asleep standing, he was so weary. How could Grey Eagle look so imposing and sound so fierce after five weeks of eating roots, berries, and nuts and sleeping in a house where the cold northwest wind blew in and out like an honored guest who must not be silenced?

"If we must," he said under his breath. He reached for Grey Hawk's fringed deerskin robe, hoping to catch him off-balance and throw him with his hip, but his opponent was much too fast and too strong. Eagle Owl felt his neck snap back; the world spun over, with the sky at his feet and the green earth overhead, and he lay on his back with no air to breathe. Grey Hawk had flipped him like a child. He had just enough strength to roll away and get to his knees before Grey Hawk had him in his powerful hands again. He was thrown to the ground face first. Grey Hawk climbed on top of him, pulling back one arm as he yanked hard on Eagle Owl's hair. The pain brought tears to his eyes. Grey Hawk's hisses filled his ear. He had one free hand and twisted to grab hold of Grey Hawk's ear; he pulled hard, Grey Hawk howled. For a second, he was free.

Eagle Owl rolled to his feet and saw blood streaming from Grey Hawk's ear. He had pulled off an earring and torn a ragged path through Grey Hawk's earlobe. He was sorry, but had no time to apologize—Grey Hawk screamed and charged him like a mad boar. Eagle Owl danced to one side, tripped the charging fighter, and fell on top of him. He heard a deep thunk and wondered why Grey Hawk lay still. Was it a trick? He was afraid to release his grip on Grey Hawk's neck and head. Slowly he let loose; the other boy did not stir. Eagle Owl got to his feet and rolled him over. At once he saw what had happened: Grey Hawk had fallen headfirst onto a rock. An ugly welt on his forehead grew by the moment. Was he dead? Eagle Owl bent close and heard raspy breathing. Relieved, he turned to run for the healer when a hand weakly grabbed his ankle.

"Two against one," Grey Hawk said in a whisper. His eyelids fluttered and closed.

Eagle Owl smiled, rubbing his sore neck. He spoke

with great effort, but his voice was just above a whisper. "Without the rock, I would have no neck."

"And no wife."

After a few moments of silence, Grey Hawk got slowly to his feet and withdrew, holding his head as if his brains might fall out. If the priest and the werowance agreed, the wedding between Quiet Lark and Eagle Owl would take place. If he could move ever again ...

🪶 🪶 🪶

The white oak leaves grew to the size of a field mouse's ear; it was time to plant corn. Women stooped over in the dirt, dropping kernels into holes and covering them before they watered the corn that would feed them for the next year. Maples were bled for sugar, which ran down in deep brown blood that stirred the children's imaginations and sweetened their bread. Men sat around the fires and sharpened their knives and hatchets, weapons they had acquired in trade with the English.

One night early in the new moon, Eagle Owl joined his father in their house. A messenger of the great chief Opechancanough stood inside. Eagle Owl was stunned by what he had come to tell them.

"Four years ago our mamanatowick Powhatan died. His half-brother Opechancanough and all Pamunkeys mourned and honored him. Thirty tribes mourned and honored his passing. Drought followed, and the deer died. Famine and fever killed many of the people. We traded land to the intruders for food, foolish men who would all have died but for our kindness and our help. Now, Powhatan's half-brother rules, and he has decreed this: We will slay all the intruders on the morning of the equinox, at the given hour. The forts will burn; the tobacco fields and the ships will burn. Nothing will remain of the intruders but their footsteps!"

Eagle Owl's mouth would not close. It was as if the man had announced that the sun would not rise in the morning. All the intruders dead? The women and children?

His friend, the skinny berry-picker with blue eyes, dead? Must it be?

After the man had been fed and had hurried back up-river to his village, Eagle Owl lingered to talk with his father long into the night. Great Eagle's face was long, and he rubbed his tired eyes. The smoke of the fire bothered him. They both coughed. He listened as Eagle Owl spoke.

"But we will trick them, father, like wicked spirits."

"We trick them to win back our land. We trick them to live our lives. Our mamanatowick promised the intruders that the sky would fall sooner than the peace be broken between us. I tell you: the sky has fallen."

Eagle Owl glanced outside. It was a strange night, grey and overcast, with no hint of the moon.

"Our ways are best," his father went on, "We know this land. It is ours. The intruders have been given too much. They have been told to leave. We have been too kind, like old women. They war upon our spirits. Now we end it."

With nothing more to say, he asked leave of his father and ran to his mother's house. Oholasc held him, and he vowed to do what he must do, as a man. That night he dreamed of being a rope stretched between the English boy and his father; they tugged from opposite ends until he broke. His blood flowed like a river and choked the crops growing in the fields. His mother wiped his brow; before awakening, he crumbled into dust and blew away in a stiff westerly wind.

He awoke with his mother wiping his forehead. "You are feverish."

"Our secret is feverish."

He left the yehawkin and followed the powerful but unseen pull of the temple. With the old healer, he passed the day in and out of the sweat lodge on the banks of the stream, driving away all visions of doubt. The heated stones gave off a dry heat that opened and cleaned a man's skin. The aches in his bones would soon disappear, he knew. The mats he sat upon were soft, and when he sat up straight, his head almost touched the roof. The lodge was comfortable and cozy; it was a dry, hot womb from which a man might be born once more. After greeting him warmly, the priest had gathered and heated four large, smooth stones in a roaring fire until they were red hot. He laid them in the center of the lodge and set upon the glowing rocks a paste of white oak bark. Namontack then closed the door. Eagle Owl felt as if he were sitting in the fiery heart of the Sun, so intense was the heat. In a short while, the priest pulled open the reed mat, letting in fresh cool air, and sprinkled Eagle Owl with cool water. The water sizzled on the rocks and sent up a shower of steam.

Eagle Owl emerged from the domed house with a clarity of vision and a lighter step. The cross given him by the young intruder burned upon his chest. He tore it off and cast it into the coals of the fire. It gave no light and made no sound but was swallowed whole and gone. He took a deep breath, smelling the river and the woods and the sweet scent of rich black earth, and ducked back into the sweat lodge for another brief period of cleansing.

He stepped out of the sweat lodge at dusk and walked to the river to bathe with the other men. The water was cool and clear; fish jumped and splashed just a few feet from him. He splashed the water on his chest and arms and dunked himself, holding his breath underwater. When he burst into the air, the first breath he took was like his first breath ever, and the world around him shone like the First Day, bathed in a soft yellow light, like gold.

He clambered up the muddy banks and watched the sun set over his shoulder. The darkness was final. A horned owl shrieked like a demon overhead. Two raccoons squabbled over fish at the water's edge. A beaver splashed his tail in alarm, warning Eagle Owl to leave his domain.

He ran back to the village to pray at the temple, where the dead werowances and priests lay resting in honor. The old priest smiled at him and rested his hand on Eagle Owl's shoulder. In the old man's eyes a fire burned; Eagle Owl's heart was seared by the priest's magic, and he had no memory of the huskanaw or of the skinny intruder with the bucket of berries, or of anything but his bow and arrows and what he could do with them.

At his house, he found bear's oil and rubbed it over his arms and legs, everywhere he could reach. The oil soothed his skin and closed the pores so that lice and fleas would not bother him as he slept. His skin shone like a lesser god's.

Tomorrow he and his people would change the world, with Okewas's help. So will it be. So must it be.

At dawn he awoke fresh and strong. He bathed in the river with the other men, who said nothing of the burning secret consuming their hearts.

Eagle Owl took his bow and arrows into the woods and shot a squirrel from a branch, piercing the squirrel's neck cleanly. He brought it back to the village and sat by the fire with the other men, who ate heartily of the fish they had caught that day. Grey Hawk stared into his eyes for a long moment, and they both smiled. Boyhood was behind them; they were men who would soon be warriors. There was no greater honor for a man.

Today they would join other men of legend and song; today and for days beyond number, they would be remembered.

Chapter Nine

THE MASSACRE

Thomas awoke with a start. There was shouting and panic in the air. Was a hailstorm brewing? He heard the rumble of distant thunder and peered outside; the sun was just over the horizon, a shimmering orange hovering above the river to the east. It was Good Friday, March 22, 1622. Thomas wasn't much for dates but the Minister was, and his last sermon emphasized again and again the solemn nature of Good Friday, when Jesus died upon the cross for the sins of all Mankind, saved and unsaved. The day offered hope to all repentants, no matter how lost. The Reverend Wilson would soon offer a special prayer, pleading for forgiveness in honor of the Great Sacrifice of Our Lord and Savior.

"I believe in the Father Almighty, Maker of Heaven and earth," they would begin, reciting the creed together, as one. Thomas wondered for a moment about Priscilla, once the only young and pretty woman in all of Jamestown. Now she was gone, one day's brisk canoeing downriver. He missed her smile and the glint of sunlight in her hair. He wanted to ask her pardon, if he had failed her. Her honeyed voice soothed and inflamed him at once — how was that possible? If only his father were more defiant of convention and had taken her in as their servant. Other planters and artisans had female servants of Priscilla's age and younger living with them. Surely they were not all sinners. If only they had the money to pay her! And what of Matthew Garret? Whose head was he bashing in at this moment? Was he guarding Priscilla as he swore to?

As Thomas put on his shirt and pulled on his boots, his father was already in the doorway wiping the sleep from his eyes. He ducked outside to talk to a militia man dashing past. Thomas was sleepy and grumpy, and his whole body itched from bedbug bites. The tallow candle on the table was just a stub, the wick no bigger than an eyelash. He missed his mother again. What could he offer Matthew's mother in exchange for more candles? The cottage was filthy and bug-ridden and needed a thorough cleaning. Thomas despised such labor and avoided it until his father threatened a beating.

Cool, fresh air entered their house and swept away the lingering stale odors of last night's stew. Thomas ran to the door and asked his father what had happened.

"Get the musket. There's talk of savages killing English folk up and down the river. Get the musket!"

Thomas's hand shook as he grabbed the musket in the corner and ran to hand it to his father, who looked up and down the streets as if danger were very near. Following his father, Thomas ran to the western palisades and climbed the hill to the cannon, which was manned and ready to fire on the earthen bulwark. The woods just a hundred feet beyond the wall suddenly appeared ominous and alive with bloodthirsty eyes. Thomas overheard his father inquire about the savages.

Johnson, a lean eighteen-year-old servant indentured to Gentleman Crofts for five more years, nodded and spoke in shaky tones. "Chanco the Indian warned his master at Pace's Paines early this very morning. Said his soul was tormented and his tongue on fire once he received the body of Christ. Said all the savages in Virginia was in revolt and bound to slaughter us like pigs this very morning."

Other men had gathered with their muskets, shooing the women and children inside the cottages. Many had gathered in the storehouse. In case of siege, extra foodstuffs were stored inside the great wooden building. Two stocky burgesses, duly elected representatives of the colony and men of power and wealth, ducked in to see that all was well and dashed out again, scurrying in their finery to gather their weapons and to secure all entrances to the fort. Nearby, inside the chapel, the Reverend Wilson led a handful of ill and disabled men in prayer and soothed a terrified widow. Thomas overheard the minister, who was torn between Christian forgiveness and English anger, as he prayed: "We know, Almighty and Merciful God, that the Devil and all the gates of Hell stand against us, but if thou, O Lord, stand with us, we care not who be against us. May our light so shine against the darkness of the heathen, that they see our good works as the sun and so be brought to glorify Thee, our heavenly Father. We have built warm nests, like the English sparrows, and we put our lives in Thy Hand. Bless us further, we dare to beseech Thee, and prosper our proceedings so that the heathen never dare to ask, 'Where is thy God now?' Blessed be God, and blessed be the King and Prince of England, and blessed be the English nation and its colonies and provinces." The Reverend paused, his cheeks flushed and working like a smith's forge, before closing with prayers. "In Romans twelve, nineteen, it is written: 'Dearly beloved, avenge not yourselves, but rather give place unto wrath: for it is written, Vengeance is mine; I will repay, saith the Lord.'" He paused to calm a recent widow, who wailed as the cannon fired again, shaking the earth and rattling the walls of the chapel. The roar deafened them and seemed to suck the air out of the building for a moment. The Reverend blinked, swallowed, and read further. "In Luke six, thirty-five, it says: 'Love ye your enemies, and do good, and lend, hoping for nothing again; and your reward shall be great, and ye shall be the children of the Highest; for he is kind unto the unthankful and to the evil.' So it is written, and so shall it be. Let us pray for a forgiveness to take root in our hearts and fill our chests with the mighty power of prayer, amen."

The Jamestown militia was forming in the square, beneath the green lace of a great elm tree. Their faces were grim, and every man checked his powder and firing caps. "What about the plantations up- and downriver?" Thomas's father asked.

Thomas Cowper, the man standing next to him, was a barber as well as a planter. He knew every man within thirty miles of the fort. "Nobody knows nothing. The only men gone upriver haven't come back."

"No word downriver from Martin's Hundred," said another.

Thomas started. That's where Priscilla was sent, and where Matthew had sworn to follow her. A force of twenty armed men had gathered, each man given a smoothbore musket as tall as Thomas, a cartridge belt, and several pounds of shot and powder carried in a leather bag around the waist. Some of the men carried pistols and swords in their belts. At the captain's order, they ran to defend the gates and to reinforce the men standing ready by the cannons. A whoop!

"Savages!"

Thomas peered over the spikes and saw them in the woods outside the fort, creeping forward, a dozen bronzed warriors holding bows and dressed in hides. The captain gave the order, the fuse was lighted, and one of the three cannons boomed. The Powhatans drew back, scattering into the woods. Muskets fired, and the smoke drifted up and over the palisades before dissipating. From the far side of the fort, where the river ran near, another cannon boomed, and they heard shouts of alarm. The eight-foot long black cannon the captain of the militia called "the murderer" thundered from the third corner of the fort, the main gate and watchtower, almost three hundred feet away. Trees fell and crashed in the cannonball's path.

Thomas raised his head above the sharpened tops of the fort walls and saw the savages holding their ground, threatening the score of houses outside the palisades. They howled like beasts and sent a volley of arrows into the fort. His father shoved him back and under a bench. Chickens squawked and roosters cock-a-dooed and ran in circles. Thomas thought them comical in their terror until one arrow pierced a chicken and it fell dead to the ground. The fowl's blood was as red as his own.

"Get down!" his father shouted at him. "Show some sense, son!"

Thomas had not seen his Indian friend and wondered where he was. He could not be a part of this treachery, could he? Another cannon bellowed from the river, and the smoke wafted across the water like a cloud. Thomas watched, mesmerized. This was the greatest show of his life, a performance not to be missed.

Shouts and hurrahs!

"The savages are withdrawn!" the captain cried.

Governor Wyatt appeared, scowling. The Governor wore a soldier's helmet and carried a fine sword that glinted in the sun. A leather breastplate covered his midsection. He nodded and pointed to the scurrying Indians, who ran deeper into the woods and vanished.

"Not one man was lost. Good work!" the Governor said. "I fear that without doubt, either we must clear the savages of the land or they us out of this country." He withdrew with his soldiers, eager to review the men guarding the cannons at the other two bulwarks.

The militia had gathered in the square before the chapel for orders. In half an hour, his father returned. "Stay here, in the storehouse with the others," he told Thomas. "I'm going downriver."

Thomas argued, but his father handed him to the minister, who vowed to watch the boy. The Reverend Wilson led them to the storehouse and offered a prayer for dry weather, so the muskets would fire. A score of men entered their canoes. Carrying muskets and powder, they paddled downriver in the lazy current. When they had vanished from sight, Thomas and the others jumped at the slightest noise. He had seen the Indians at close hand and had no illusions about besting them in combat. He prayed that the fighting would end and that his father would survive the trouble. The thought struck him that of all the folks he knew, only the Berry Thief had the courage to explore the mountains with him and perhaps to show him where the gold lay. He thought again of Willis and Tillman, the adventurers who had spurned his offer of help and were never heard from again. How did they die? Had they found gold?

As the minister bowed his head in prayer, Thomas slipped off and hid by the barrels of gunpowder just inside the main gate. He bided his time and watched carefully, until a group of twelve men left the fort at noon, scouting the woods for savages. When the gate opened, he dashed past the men, who called to him to stop, and ran to the river. He uncovered a canoe hidden under branches on the muddy shore. Ignoring shouts to halt, he paddled furiously, his spine stiffening when he realized that he had no weapon and no food. If the savages caught him again, he would be at their mercy, and from what he had heard, they had little of that on this most wicked of Good Fridays. Yet he had to find Priscilla, and he feared losing his father and being orphaned.

The sun warmed his face, and the breeze cooled his brow as his arms pumped. He drank river water but ate nothing, paddling all afternoon with the sluggish current before pulling the canoe to a muddy bank as darkness fell. Exhausted, his arms aching, he prayed for protection and fell asleep in the grass beneath a broad weeping willow, the crickets' songs ringing in his ears.

He paddled downriver for half of the next day, ducking for cover when a boat approached. He saw armed Englishmen but no Indians. In the afternoon, he heard pops of musket fire and shouts from the shore but saw no one until he came to the southern outskirts of Martin's Hundred, the tobacco plantation he had heard of but never seen. He paddled ashore and hid the canoe among the vines and weeds choking the shoreline.

He crept up the path and ducked when he heard a shout.

"Who's there?"

Thomas stood and identified himself. It was Harris, the cobbler. The man cursed him. "I might have shot you, boy! You're a fool!"

The scene Thomas stumbled upon turned his stomach. The bodies of men, women, and children lay across the earth as if Satan had stolen up through the bowels of the earth to snuff out each life. Their heads were crushed or split open; blood flowed in pools on the earth. Thomas saw his father doubled over in pain at the far side of the field, near the house. No smoke escaped from the chimney. Stepping past his father, who did not look up, Thomas stood in the doorway and looked inside the house. Pewter tankards and a fresh loaf of bread rested on a large table.

In the corner, a cedar chest with its lid raised suggested an open mouth. The cooking fire had long since burned itself out. Suspended above the coals was an iron cooking pot with spoiled venison stew; the smell was revolting. Thomas almost gagged. There was no sign of violence in the manor house, and an eerie peace yet inhabited the building, which had a wood floor and stairs up to the second floor. It was the grandest house Thomas had seen in Virginia. Would anyone dare to live there again?

The savages hadn't stepped inside but caught the English outside at work, or lured them outside on some pretence. The tobacco barn had burned to the ground, and two charred bodies lay inside like charcoal-men from a terrifying fairy tale. Thomas could not look at them. The fields had been set ablaze and had burned to blackened stumps; as far as Thomas could see lay acres of the charred stubs of tobacco plants. The air reeked of death and smoke. The wanton destruction angered him. No one could defend such waste.

He turned when a soft light caught his eye. The sun glinted off gleaming blonde hair beneath a plain white cap; Thomas knew at once that it was Priscilla Powell. He ran to her and found her asleep. Her face was composed. A savage had shattered her skull with an axe. Taken by surprise, she died without agony. Thomas withdrew, almost stepping on a hand. Gold and silver coins lay scattered about the ground like trinkets of no value. The savages had no use for them; they sought revenge, not wealth. By a stream he spied the neatly severed head of a boy younger than he; the look of horror and agony on the boy's face made Thomas wretch. All around him, men with shovels were burying bodies, but the work seemed to go on endlessly. He heard someone say wearily, "Seventy. Seventy of them dead."

Thomas looked closer at one bloodstained body and saw Matthew, his nose broken and one eye gouged out, lying in a pool of his own blood. His mouth was open, but he would never say another unkind word. Thomas reached to do something, to offer some comfort to the simple and heartsick boy who deserved nothing like this, when a tall shadow fell over him and he froze.

At the touch of his father on his sleeve, Thomas jumped. "I told you to stay in the fort, son. What good does it do if you're killed?"

Thomas jumped to his feet and hugged his father; tears filled his eyes and fell into his lips. "He loved her, father."

His father held him tightly. Other men wept openly; some collapsed upon the earth and were sick. The captain quickly ordered a a prayer service for all the dead and a "return to the protection of the fort forthwith." They all dug graves until their arms ached and their hands bled, using shovels they found in the tool shed. Thomas was numbed by the death and disfigurement. His heart hardened against the savages who had done this terrible deed, but he could weep no more for Priscilla, who would never again tease and befuddle him, or for Matthew. He would miss them both terribly, for there were few others their age who were free to do as they chose. The indentured servants his age were glum or wicked or stupid; he felt no kinship with them. For a moment he thought of the savage who had given him the gold nugget and his heart leapt; then he recalled where he was, and what he held in his hands, and the shovel was heavy with dirt and grief. He could never befriend the savage again. He must kill the boy if he saw him. Could he kill him? Could he kill anyone? What if the Berry Thief and his kin were not responsible for the bloodbath? There were many different tribes, Thomas knew, and no Englishman since John Smith could tell them apart. No, it did not matter. It was too late. He and the others who stood beside him with shovels could never again be friends with any Indian.

Having completed their gruesome task, they paddled back upriver, easily besting the weary current. The men jerked their muskets in the direction of every snap of a twig. They saw no one alive, neither savage nor English. Thomas shut his eyes and saw blood—and Priscilla Powell's last smile.

✤ ✤ ✤

At the storage shed beside the village storehouse, the Jamestown militia met to organize a punitive party to search out and kill the offending savages. Blessed by the minister, who read a verse from Scripture and spoke of God's wrath, the men shuffled their feet and kept their eyes downcast.

"Our sins have brought this judgment down upon us," the Reverend Wilson began. He pointed a finger at the gentlemen in the crowd, and they returned glares that might have silenced a lesser preacher, or a wiser one, for they paid his wages. "Sins! Finery, excessive apparel, gold threads and silver buckles. Vanity of vanities, all is vanity! Gluttony and drunkenness on the Sabbath. Do you see where they lead? Sins and vices. Go now and sin no more!"

The men departed grimly, armed to the teeth. All work ceased in the fields. The people of Jamestown would have to live on the food they grew in their gardens and what they had already gathered in the storehouse. Men who went out alone or in small parties did not return. The two men who had left to find gold were not heard from either, they who had sworn to "conquer the mountains and all of China!" Thomas feared the worst. But for his father and the minister, it seemed that everyone he knew was either dead or gone. He held out little hope for the future. He looked ahead and foresaw bloodshed, fear, and a struggle against the Indians and the earth and sky to grow a crop they could not eat. Their sacrifice made so little sense.

He spoke to his father that night about returning to England. His father spat on the floor.

"You're thinking of the glassmakers, the Poles and Germans who cracked the furnace with a crow bar on purpose and were sent back home."

Thomas nodded; he envied the dark bearded men who spoke a musical language that sounded like a child's nonsense song to him. Though they had failed and produced nothing for the village but grief, they were home now, surrounded by their families. As far as Thomas knew, there were no savages in Poland or Germany. They were safe in their beds. They had food and sweethearts, he would wager.

"We are through with England, son. She'll not have us back, 'cept as paupers. I'd sooner starve here. I'll not leave your mother either, or your brother."

Thomas drew back and thought about his father's words; the argument made sense to him. Six weeks inside the bowels of the pitching ship was as close to Hell as Thomas ever hoped to come. He bade his father a good night but slept fitfully, arising when he heard shouts from within the walls. A false alarm, but every man in the village was out the door with his musket, running for the gate and the walls and the cannons.

The next morning, shouts and gunfire awoke him. Smoke drifted aimlessly across the water like acrid clouds. Thomas arose and ran to the gates and saw a majestic pinnace, a great ship with billowing canvas sails making her way into port. The English flag snapped in the breeze. Hurrahs! Men and women crowded the decks to wave and give thanks. Their eyes were wide with wonder: so this is the New World, they were thinking. It is green and lush!

Thomas joined the others and ran to greet them. On deck, a pale, handsome new Comer in a plumed hat and tight waistcoat produced silk, offering to swap a pound of the fine fabric for fifty pounds of tobacco.

"I've got the worms and a mulberry tree!" a Jamestowner shouted back.

"But you have no silk!"

The high spirits were short-lived. Governor Wyatt arrived with six armed men and called for the ship to unload its cargo—linens, gunpowder, muskets, hogs and cattle, a pair of horses, three mastiffs, goats, and chickens—immediately. Panic spread among those families and men aboard ship who had endured six weeks at sea to set foot on paradise and were now told that a slaughter of English folk was underway. Word of the massacre spread quickly, and celebrations were postponed. The ship was unloaded under heavy guard, and the goods carried inside the walls of the fort with all due haste. Every man helped. Thomas spied a boy of his height, a boy he might have befriended, but there was such great fear in his rabbit eyes that Thomas felt pity and let the boy be. The frightened new Comer clung to his mother's skirt like a fool. They all scurried for cover inside the high walls of the fort, and many wept and cried aloud for pardon and protection. Reverend Wilson ran to succor them, and his prayers rang through the village for hours, until hunger demanded a respite, and they all ate bread and eggs and drank cold well water, struggling to contain their fear. Children would not leave their mothers' laps, and grown men shook in the knees as they were handed muskets and shown how to fire them.

That night, Thomas slept deeply, dreaming of the Berry Thief's rough cottage in the woods. The savage met him with a smile and offered Thomas a staff that turned into a copperhead, which struck without warning, puncturing Thomas's neck. He lay writhing in pain while the savage laughed an echoing demon's laugh, bitter and cruel, as mad a sound as a hoot owl screeching in the darkest stretch of woods in all the New World.

◆　◆　◆

Thomas awoke bathed in sweat and breathing hard. He could hear the wails of the new Comers, and from the woods the harrowing call of a night bird, or a savage imitating one. He and his father and the others hiding behind the palisades were no match for the Powhatans or the woods or the beasts, he feared. They were lost in a lost land, and they would surely lose their grip on the land one day, and no trace of them would ever be found. Like Raleigh's Lost Colony, they were doomed to be mocked and mourned in the blink of history's eye and then forgotten, as men overwhelmed by circumstance or ill fortune should be forgotten, for they had failed.

He fell asleep again praying for peace and for the repose of his mother's soul. At some point, he heard his father whimper, just once, like a boy whose favorite wooden toy had been snatched away. He opened his eyes for a moment and caught a glimpse of his father curled up in

bed and twitching like a dog dreaming his way down a
rabbit hole. Not wanting to see his father like that, Thomas
turned away. His heart was as heavy as his eyes, which had
seen too much, he feared, for a boy of fourteen summers.
He shut his eyes and prayed for sleep to take him away to
a land of peace.

In his dream his mother's hazel eyes smiled at him,
and his baby brother walked beneath a flowering apple
tree. With his father's laughter ringing through the clear air
like a bell, Thomas fed them all golden pears the size of
church bells, and he alone could look up and see the white-
winged angels hovering over the family, protecting and
blessing them all, forever and ever, amen.

🐟   🐟   🐟

Early the next morning, Thomas awoke as the grey light of
dawn stretched slowly over the village. The fire in the
hearth was out; it was chilly for a spring morning. He rose
with a blanket wrapped around him and went to the door,
listening for shouts of warning. He heard a bird chirp and
opened the door a crack, peering out. No plummeting arrows in sight. In the dusty path in front of their cottage, a
robin pulled at a worm squirming to crawl back into a
hole. The robin won the struggle and swallowed the worm,
tilting back its head. Thomas had to laugh—the early bird
got the worm. His laughter startled the robin; the orange-
breasted bird flew off to its mud and grass nest beside a
neighbor's cottage. As the pale daylight brightened, Thomas squinted, watching as the mother robin spewed the half-
digested worm into the bills of two paler, spotted robin
chicks. Like the lilies of the field, God provided for them.
Thomas had to have faith, trust in God and the King and
the men of Jamestown to prevail. There was no other an-
swer; he had no mother to run to, no friends—only his father, who sometimes thought his son a fool or a rogue. He
had to please his father, to pray for victory over heathens,
and to bury his dreams of gold and wealth. To survive: that
was the challenge fate threw at his feet. His goal must be

life, not wealth; to breathe and to sing, and one day to walk with a pretty girl along the banks of the river, happy as otters.

Thomas heard a rustle of clothing and a groan from within the cottage. He turned and shut the door behind him. From the barn, a cock crowed, and the cow mooed. Indians or no, the animals were hungry. Thomas took a step toward his bedstead where his boots lay as his father cleared his throat and sat up in bed. In the shadows, he appeared insubstantial, more imagined than real.

"Thomas," his father said softly and in a hoarse voice, "I was dreaming of your mother ..." He could say no more without tears and bit his lip as he got to his feet. Thomas ran to him and hugged him, feeling his father's muscles jump beneath his shirt as he embraced his son. Thomas held onto his father tightly, breathlessly. His father's affection was worth almost any sorrow.

"Bolt the door, son, lest this fine moment be our last."

Thomas hesitated. "It's a quiet morning."

"It was quiet Friday, before they struck."

Thomas did as he was told and revealed his dream, as much as he could remember, to his father, who nodded in understanding as he built a fire. "I miss your mother, too, and your brother," he said simply, not looking up from the flaming reeds and kindling in the fireplace. "Feed the animals, Thomas."

Outside, wood smoke hung in the air. The villagers of Jamestown were rising to the day; fear would not keep them prisoners inside their mean cottages any longer. In the lean-to barn, the chickens and cows scolded Thomas with clucks and lows of disapproval. He shivered and scattered the corn, humming a hymn to himself.

After a breakfast of biscuits and tea, Thomas shouldered the hoe and rake, his father the musket, powder, and shot. With a party of twelve other planters and their servants, they left the safety of the fort and marched two abreast toward the green tobacco fields. The morning dew glistened in the grass. Thomas flinched with each snap of a twig and every rustle of the leaves. The walk seemed endless, as if every other step took them backwards and they were getting nowhere. With the silence of the cannons, the cowbirds and cardinals had returned to the trees, and the forest was in song.

At the sight of the tobacco fields, the party of armed men halted in silence. The tobacco seedlings had been mutilated, torn from the earth and stomped. Planters muttered their sorrow or cursed the savages. Charles Spencer raised a hand to silence them. "We have done the same to their fields."

Thomas was amazed that his father had said that. One planter reminded his father that the savages had started the war, but Thomas thought to ask: Whose land was it first? He looked to his father, who bowed his head as if in church, and said nothing for a moment. The others waited to see what he wanted to do. Thomas thought they might return to the fort and give up on this year's crop.

His father sighed, leaning on the musket at his side. His voice was firm. "We'll plant new seedlings." He tore at the weeds and shaped the tobacco mounds with care, glancing over his shoulder toward the woods as the other men did. Two men with muskets stood guard, searching the edge of the woods for any movement. Soon they had worked up a sweat under the glare of a hot April sun. Thomas almost welcomed the blisters on his palms. He felt pleased and fortunate to be working beside his father in their fields and hoped they would both survive to harvest the gold leaf tobacco that had almost cost them their lives.

🪶 🪶 🪶

Standing in the doorway of their cottage at twilight, Thomas sensed his father drawing near to him. He smelled the green life of the fields in his father, and the sweat of his labor. His father's hand was solid as oak on his shoulder. He spoke so softly that he almost whispered. "We will prevail, son. We have a thousand years of history behind us. These savages are demons, true. They will never again be trusted. Don't you worry; we'll drive them west, over the mountains and into the sea, if that's what it takes to make this land safe. We've beaten the French and the Moors and the Spanish; no red man with a tomahawk is about to chase us off this land, not now or ever. I swear it."

Thomas could not remember when his father had spoken so fervently of anything but tobacco. He felt a surge of pride and power. Yet dread and fear refused to surrender their grip on his heart. "What about Raleigh and the lost colony? And Martin's Hundred?" Thomas was also thinking of Priscilla Powell and Matthew Garret, dead at his age. The Indians were powerful enemies, clever and deadly. They fought as Englishmen never would, using treachery and stealth. He thought of the Eagle-boy, the Indian, with a rush of regret and pain. Thomas wished he had only dreamt about the blood and gore of the massacre, but it was real. Perhaps one day far in the future, they might meet again, and in Christian forgiveness greet one another, trade gold nuggets for hatchets, and speak of their sorrows and dreams in a language yet unspoken, a language of their own, a dream-tongue known only to each other. He flushed, guilty at the thought—however wild—of befriending an Indian. At the chapel on the Sunday after the massacre, the minister had spoken of "generations of fear and hate" before peace with the Powhatans was possible. How many years was that, Thomas wondered. Forty? Fifty? Imagine a hundred years of fear and hate. What people could bear that burden?

His father stood beside him in the doorway. They watched as two new Comers, a man and his wife, scurried past carrying buckets of well water. Their faces were hard with fear. Thomas felt the firm flesh of his father's arm as he encircled his son in a protective embrace. "We have gunpowder, the English crown, and the Hand of God on our side. We won't fail. We won't be fooled again."

Thomas nodded. He understood.

His father had more to say; Thomas could hardly fathom all the words that tumbled out of his father's usually solemn, tight mouth. "Your son and your son's son will walk this land and plow these fields, and in peace. That is the only promise I'll ever make to you, son, and it will be kept by me and men like me, do you understand?"

Thomas formed the word "Yes," but it would not come out of his mouth. He understood, and he believed. A cock crowed, and overhead a vast body of pigeons flew past, more than anyone could count. The bounty of this land!

The setting sun cast a crimson blanket over the earth. A breeze in from the river carried the moist promise of growth and abundance, and the sweet stink of fish and mud and scum. Inside the smoky cottage, they ate in silence until his father asked Thomas a riddle, the first time he had done so since their arrival in the new world.

"What did the cricket say to the sad ladybug?" Charles asked, his eyebrows raised in amusement.

Thomas shrugged. He had no experience with riddles. He felt an unfamiliar tickle in his throat.

"Cheer-up, cheer-up," his father said, in imitation of the cricket's call.

Thomas laughed until he choked. They both laughed, dropping their spoons and throwing back their heads. Their laughter rose like tolling bells pealing the joy of life on this earth.

Chapter Ten

WANDERING WARRIORS

Little Dove and Quiet Lark stood arm in arm in the chilling drizzle and wept; the children stood by them, holding a hem of their deerskin skirts. Little Dove's dead husband lay on the ground before them, wrapped in skins and mats, his bead necklaces and earrings tucked inside. The stake-lined grave was shallow; they had to hurry. The intruders might come at any moment. The dead warrior was lowered into the grave by Great Eagle and three other men. The two deerskin-clad women, his wife and daughter, mourned grievously and tossed beads into the grave before the body was covered with dirt.

After the funeral, Quiet Lark and Little Dove painted their faces black to show their grief. They would not wash off the oil and dye until sunset of the following day. Great Eagle soothed them and spoke to everyone in the village of Quiyoughcohannock, recalling the dead man's bravery, his loyalty, his love for the people. He did not mention the intruder's musket ball that had pierced and shattered the fallen warrior's heart. There would be war. More men would die, but there was no need to talk of it. Children whimpered and whined as they were told that they must leave the village that had been their only home for every season but winter, when they followed the hunters.

Eagle Owl listened as Namontack took the frightened children aside and in a glade near the temple, told them of life after death. "The fields are green and ripe, and no work is needed to harvest them," the old priest began. The children wiped away tears and looked up at him expectantly.

He pointed to the sky, where a grey blanket of clouds squashed the light of the sun. "There, the people wear the finest and most rare of feathers and are painted with the purest, brightest oils and colors, and they rest in the shade and sleep in peace, and eat delicious fruits, and before them lie bottomless baskets of beads and hatchets and copper; they sing and dance and feast all day and night, and the fires always burn unattended, and all the people are watched over by the Great Hare." He paused to touch the children, who smiled and were reassured. Eagle Owl noticed with a jolt of insight that the old magic man was untouched by the rain, which had soaked everyone else. His hair and cloak were dry. How did he work such magic? "And when they age greatly like me and die, they return as children, and walk with us once again, and all give thanks and rejoice."

"Was I an old chief once?" a little boy dared to ask. "Who was I?"

Namontack reared back and laughed, showing his yellow tobacco-stained teeth. "No, little one; you were an owl who asked '... 'who' one too many times. It's time to go now."

The old priest looked back at the temple he must now abandon. He had never before appeared so weary and un-certain to Eagle Owl, who thought that the old sorcerer knew everything worth knowing and feared nothing. A run-ner from the Pamunkeys had brought word the day after the attack that the English fort had not fallen; he did not need to say more. Great Eagle's face could not hide the disappointment and the concern he felt. The Algonkians had failed to slay all the intruders, and now the Powhatans, the Pamunkeys, and all of the Algonkian Peoples faced ex-tinction; they must get to the safety of the woods and plan their attacks carefully. As werowance, Great Eagle gave the order, and everyone scurried to do his work. The green spring would pass them by as they hid like outcasts behind the high wall of woods to the west, where the Monacans threatened them as well. They would live on berries and nuts, like squirrels, and move their village with each sun-rise. They would fight. Surrender was out of the question.

Eagle Owl stood by the old priest, wondering what he might do to help. He asked, but the old man said nothing, as if he had not heard him. The reed and bark dome that had covered the raised platforms where the dead leaders lay and that sheltered the leering idol of Okewas would soon be destroyed, he knew. The supporting poles would be knocked down, and the food and gifts scattered to the four winds, and wasted. He knew that the intruders would not allow one reed of the temple to stand, that the English would gleefully desecrate the bodies of the dead werowances and smash the black idol of Okewas, the god who brought so much grief but must be heeded. The magic man's eyes were heavy. Eagle Owl feared that each time Namontack blinked, he might never again raise those heavy lids.

Eagle Owl watched as the men and women packed all they must carry—food, weapons, tools—into baskets and litters they would carry as far as need be to escape the wrath of the intruders. He wandered past the growing fields to the edge of the woods just outside the encircling palisades, where a handful of warriors carrying clubs and shields stood watch, and soon he came upon the drooping flowers of a trumpet creeper. A ruby-throated humming-bird danced in the air, whirring and fanning the air around him. Eagle Owl studied the tiny bird and wished that he could fly away and live on nectar and never feel the loss of home. Earlier, he had asked his father if their village might be spared the torch, but Great Eagle had said nothing. They would be spared no sorrow, not now.

They left together, all of them, taking a narrow twisting path that snaked west, away from the river, turning their backs on their village and their past. No one spoke; even the children were quiet. Eagle Owl watched them go, then raced toward the river.

* * *

He ducked beneath a hollow log at the sound of the in-truder's voice, which was high-pitched and hurried, like a frightened woman's. Eagle Owl slowly raised his head and saw them, two intruders who had found his hidden house and were setting it ablaze. They wore iron hats and shirts that glinted in the sun. They carried muskets. One man emerged from within the house with Eagle Owl's treasures in the worn leather bag and tossed them into the dirt, grinding them into worthless trinkets with his boot. Enraged, Eagle Owl stood and fired an arrow that struck the thief squarely in the chest. He staggered and fell, opening his mouth as if to cry out but making no sound at all. The other man turned and fired his musket. The ball whizzed by Eagle Owl's ear. The sound of the shot popped and smoke rose above the gun. He heard the shouts of other intruders, three of them. Eagle Owl ran for his life. The men sounded like mad hogs behind him, crashing through the brush. He ran to the ravine and pushed aside the sharp shiny leaves of a holly bush, vanishing into a hollowed-out log. Holding his breath, his knife drawn, he heard them as they ran past, hollering to each other and snorting like pigs. He lay there until nightfall, hardly breathing.

🔻   🔻   🔻

The night passed. In the morning, he joined his father and Grey Hawk to spy on the English river fort. Peering through the leaves by the little river's edge, Eagle Owl spied a great English boat. Her sails billowed in the breeze, puffing with pride. Four large sails, white and alive, puffed with pride in the westerly wind. Three smaller sails stood square and taut. The woodwork on the great ship struck him as perfect. How could these men too foolish to grow corn and store it safely carve wood so lovingly? The boat appeared seaworthy. It had come far, no doubt. The beauty of the boat made no sense to him.

His father gripped his arm and nodded. Women in great skirts that dragged to the ground emerged from the bowels of the boat. They looked like pale fine beings from another world stepping down here. They might have been enormous butterflies. Eagle Owl expected them to fly away over the trees. Where were their wings?

Barrels rolled off the ship and clunked down the plank. What was in them, he wondered? Food, drink, gunpowder?

Grey Hawk wanted to swim across as darkness fell, holding his bow and arrows in his teeth. Great Eagle asked him to wait, and he fell silent.

🪶 🪶 🪶

Algonkian warriors struck the intruders when they could, escaping to the cover of the woods before the English could mount a counterattack. Great Eagle led a small band of twelve men; Eagle Owl's nemesis, Grey Hawk, led the younger fighters. Great Eagle proudly wore the eagle feather that symbolized his power and station; others wore feathers in their hair, and some painted their arms and chests with three horizontal bars of bright colors. The women and children followed, guarded by six warriors and protected by the old priest's charms, which made them invisible for short periods of time. Grey Hawk's courage had earned him a new name, Necotowance; he was destined to be a leader and a great man.

Great Eagle and his followers struck the Englishmen as they entered and left their boats, as they left the fort to get fresh water or to relieve themselves, as they followed Great Eagle's trail. Ambush was their weapon, and they used it well. Most of the English fighters they killed made no sound as they died.

🪶 🪶 🪶

A week after the great attack, which had taken three hundred English lives but had failed to drive the intruders out of their land, Eagle Owl received his father's blessing and ran back to their village in search of arrowheads, knives, food — anything the intruders had neglected to destroy. A bright sun hurt his eyes; he was unaccustomed to roaming freely in the day. Charred wood now stood where the houses and temple had burned to ashes. The circle of stones that had been their hearthfire was out, for the first time in his memory. The fields were black stubble; even the crows found little to eat. Blackbirds gazed at him with stupid, puzzled eyes. Looking carefully, he found an arrowhead, then another, both made of shells. A bead necklace lay covered by ash near the sweat lodge, which had burned into ashes. He brushed off the soot and put it in his bag.

He heard the snap of a twig and dove behind a pine. Peering out, he saw nothing. Turning his head this way and that, he listened. Nothing. It must have been a doe, puzzled by the destruction. He had left his bow by the river. They needed food; the children were hungry and cried and whined all day, until they were hushed by their mothers, who feared the intruders' muskets at every snap of a twig.

With no houses and no crops, their fishing weirs smashed, and their corn taken or burned, the people moved with every sunrise, eating fish and game, nuts, unripe berries that made your stomach cry out. They bathed when they could, in small, fast-running streams, but often they were dirty and felt sorrowful.

Returning from their destroyed village, Eagle Owl saw Quiet Lark. Her face was smudged from a cooking fire, and her deerskin robe was filthy. She looked like a maiden who had fallen to the wiles of Okewas and now served the dark god. Eagle Owl was angered and yearned to strike somehow or to kill something when he saw her like that. She refused to look him in the eye. They had failed. Their people had failed; the gods no longer protected them.

Rejoining his father by a small stream, Eagle Owl showed him the arrowheads and received a pat of thanks. His father reminded him of their history and of Opechancanough's oath to drive the intruders into the sea. Moved by their suffering, Eagle Owl swore allegiance to him and the people. His father was proud, yet he could not smile; there was too much suffering and sadness.

That night, Eagle Owl dreamed that he could see through his flesh and into his own heart—a stone heart cold and still in his chest. He awoke but the stone heart was so heavy, he could not move. When he opened his mouth to cry out for help, the stone held back his tongue. He pressed his hand to the stone heart and it warmed, slowly at first, like the stones in the sweat lodge, until the heart burst, spewing ashes and dust. Eagle Owl jumped to his feet and danced in triumph. He had no heart, but he could move and fight.

When he awoke before sunrise, his father's hand was on his shoulder. He got up and followed his father to the mist-enshrouded little river near the fort. Across the slow-flowing water the eerie sounds of an intruder raising his voice in song came to them, like a lullaby. His voice was sweet and high to any ears. Eagle Owl and his father listened. When the song ended, he watched as his father notched an arrow, and he did the same. When he pulled back the bow and released the arrow, it sailed with a perfect arc, a whirring rainbow, a bridge through the air to the other side, where it may have hit something. At first there was no cry of alarm or pain.

Eagle Owl could not see where his arrow had landed. With his father, he notched another arrow and pulled back the bow. The song had ended, and the intruders' cries of alarm, which arose sharply and suddenly, were familiar to him. The cries were music he understood. Again, the release, the arc, the rainbow in the air, the bridge from bow to target, the movement from his hand to the flesh of the enemy.

If he hit something, so be it. It was time to string another arrow, to pull back the bow, to let fly. May the gods guide it where they would have it go. *Twang!* The bow sang again, the arrow soared like an eagle, and his heart beat faster.

BIBLIOGRAPHY

Your local library and favorite bookstore are sure to have many books about Jamestown and the Powhatans worth reading. Below are my favorites, the books I found most useful and interesting in discovering what life was really like back then. I've also noted some books that are easy to read and full of adventure as a starting point for those who want to ease their way into the past.

GOOD BOOKS TO BEGIN WITH

Pocahontas, by Laurence Santrey (Mahwah, New Jersey: Troll Associates, 1985).

Thirty-two pages, with wonderful color illustrations by David Wenzel. Easy to read and fun! Why did she save John Smith?

Jamestown, New World Adventure, by James E. Knight (Mahwah, New Jersey: Troll Associates, 1982).

Thirty pages, easy to read, and with black and white art by Mr. Wenzel. A diary of one man's struggle to survive in the New World.

MORE CHALLENGING BOOKS ABOUT JAMESTOWN

Everyday Life in Early America, by David Freeman Hawke (New York: Harper and Row, 1988).

Almost 200 pages of fascinating facts about real life in the 1600s, both in Virginia and up north in Massachusetts, where the Pilgrims settled. For example, why did so many fires burn down entire villages? Because the first chimneys were made of wood! (I'm not kidding.)

The Old Dominion in the Seventeenth Century, edited by Warren M. Billings (Chapel Hill: University of North Carolina Press, 1975).

Funny, wild, and touching firsthand accounts of life in the 1600s, written by the people who lived then. Journals, records, and songs!

MORE CHALLENGING BOOKS ABOUT THE POWHATANS

America 1585: The Complete Drawings of John White, by Paul Hulton (Chapel Hill: University of North Carolina Press, 1984).

Almost 200 pages of beautiful color and black and white art of the Indians fishing and hunting in the late sixteenth century. A stunning book to look at, and interesting to read. White drew these pictures 400 years ago!

Indians in Seventeenth Century Virginia, by Ben C. McCary (Charlottesville: University Press of Virginia, 1957).

Less than 100 pages, this book is full of details about Indian rituals in life and death. Well worth a read!

The Powhatan Indians of Virginia: Their Traditional Culture, by Helen C. Rountree (Norman: University of Oklahoma Press, 1989).

Over 200 pages of priceless information about the Powhatans, who never wrote things down (their culture was instead oral and aural). The author brings the Powhatans to life as a people of dignity and distinction.

The Powhatan Tribes, by Christian F. Feest (New York: Chelsea House Publishers, 1990).

Just over 100 pages long, this valuable book is chock full of art and stirring accounts of Powhatan life from "aboriginal" times (before the English arrived in Virginia) through today. A worthy, terrific book!

Many other worthwhile books about Jamestown and the Powhatans (and Pocahontas!) are waiting at your library. Check them out!

DID YOU ENJOY THIS BOOK?
Check these Compelling Titles from Shoe Tree

The Admiral and the Deck Boy: One Boy's Journey with Christopher Columbus, by Genevieve A. O'Connor. Ages 10 and up. Historical Fiction. 168 pages, 6x9, illustrations, glossary. 1-55870-218-0, $12.95, hardcover.

Cadets at War: The True Story of Teenage Heroism at the Battle of New Market, by Susan Provost Beller. Ages 8-12. History. 96 pages, 6x9, photographs, maps, index. 1-55870-196-6, $9.95, hardcover.

With Secrets to Keep, by Rose Levit. Ages 12 and up. Fiction. 160 pages, 6x9. 1-55870-197-4, $12.95, hardcover.

The Curtain Rises: A History of Theater from its Origins in Greece and Rome through the English Restoration, by Paula Gaj Sitarz. Ages 10-14. History. 144 pages, 8½x11, photographs, illustrations, index. 1-55870-198-2, $14.95, hardcover.

The Glory Road: The Story of Josh White, by Dorothy Schainman Siegel. Ages 12 and up. Biography. 160 pages, 5½x8½, photos, index. 1-55870-217-2, $7.95, paper.

Woman of Independence: The Life of Abigail Adams, by Susan Provost Beller. Ages 10-14. Biography. 128 pages, 5½x8½, photos, index. 1-55870-237-7, $5.95, paper.

Breaking the Chains: The Crusade of Dorothea Lynde Dix, by Penny Colman. Ages 10-14. Biography. 144 pages, 5½x8½, photos, illustrations, index. 1-55870-219-9, $5.95, paper.

Fiddler to the World: The Inspiring Life of Itzhak Perlman, by Carol H. Behrman. Ages 10-14. Biography. 128 pages, 5½x8½, photos, index. 1-55870-238-5, $5.95, paper.

Please try your favorite bookseller first. If all else fails, tell us what you want. Send the price of the book plus $2.50 for UPS shipping (any number of books) to Shoe Tree Press, P.O. Box 219, Crozet, VA 22932.